Puncture Up

COLIN WRIGHT

Asymmetrical Press
Missoula, Montana

Published by Asymmetrical Press
Missoula, Montana.

Library of Congress Cataloging-In-Publication Data
Puncture up / Colin Wright — 1st ed.
ISBN: 978-1-938793-94-3
eISBN: 978-1-938793-93-6
WC: 69,073
1. Fiction. 2. Science Fiction. 3. Simulations. 4. Universes. 5. Kinda geeky.

Cover design by Colin Wright
Formatted in beautiful Montana
Printed in the U.S.A.

Publisher info:
Website: www.asymmetrical.co
Email: howdy@asymmetrical.co
Twitter: @asympress

ASYM METR ICAL

ACKNOWLEDGEMENTS

A great big thanks to the folks who helped me whip this book into suitable shape for publication:

James Lewis, Jon Schulz, Dyan Nielsen, Lisa Figueroa, Michael Goll, Marsha Amanova, Erin Maclean, and Shawn Mihalik.

Any typos or other mistakes are probably the result of me ignoring their damn good advice.

May our creations be accurate reflections of their creators, and may we like what we see when we face them.

What we achieve inwardly will change outer reality.
—PLUTARCH

Look up at the stars and not down at your feet. Try to make sense of
what you see, and wonder about what makes the universe exist.
Be curious.
—STEPHEN HAWKING

Puncture Up

POPE

Eugene Crisp, Chief Storyteller at Proxy

It was a question that made Dr. Amelia Pope kill herself. The first time, anyway.

The question was, "What is the proper response to learning that there is, in fact, a God?"

This is the story of Dr. Pope, a company called Proxy, the quest to find a proper hook, and an answer to the aforementioned question. An answer that Dr. Pope herself gave as all of her thoughts drifted away, darkness replacing light.

Michael Hutchins, janitor at Proxy

The doctor was a really nice woman. Even us rank-and-file types, she always had a smile and a little nod for us, though you could tell she wasn't completely there with you all the time, you know? Was in her own world, thinking some great big thoughts that were occupying her mind completely.

I think what really threw people off about Dr. Pope was how cold she could be about some things when most other people would go all hot. Rather than getting all mad and what have you, she'd go very calm, very chilly.

I heard once, and I don't know if this actually happened, because I only heard it from someone else, and who knows where they heard it? But I heard once that she was run off the road by some jerk who was late to work and his wife was leaving him and he was just mad at the world, the way people get sometimes when their lives have gone sideways. Anyway, she must have cut him off or something, or at least he thought she did, and he got barking mad, honking his horn and swerving up next to her, nudging and nudging until she pulled off onto the shoulder of the highway.

Now, most people in that situation would be angry. I'd probably be ready for a fight, you know? That kind of behavior's dangerous, not to mention lawless. But Dr. Pope, she just steps up out of the car and waits for the man to storm on over to her. He shouts and yells and makes all kinds of ruckus, spit flying this way and that, his hands waving all over the damn place. And Dr. Pope, she just stands there, calm as you please.

After maybe two or three minutes of roaring and swatting around, the man's worn himself out and just stares at the doctor, waiting for her to respond in some way, to yell back, to threaten or slap or whatever else. So he can feel alive or something. But she just stands there, looking at him, no expression on her face.

It's maybe ten seconds of that before he breaks down, apologizes, and gives one of those sniffle-snorts you hear when someone is holding back pain, only to have it kind of rip them open from the inside. He starts crying and telling Dr. Pope that it's not her he's upset at, it's his soon-to-be ex-wife and his boss and whatever.

Right then, when she's got this jerk pretty much rolled over and exposing his belly, what does she do? Does she kick him? Does she break the poor man down even further?

No.

Well, then, does she pat him on the shoulder? Say, "There there, buddy, it'll be okay?" Help him feel better?

No.

She walks back to her car and drives away.

Cold as you please. Nice woman, but goddamn.

Dr. Sunder Davies, Simulation Department Head at Proxy

Oh yes. I've heard the road rage story. I don't know if it's true or not, but I wouldn't put it past her. Amelia could sometimes be as unyielding as a boulder in the winter, and about as forgiving. And she could roll right over you, too, if you got in her way once she'd made up her mind about something.

That said, she was fiercely protective of people. And not just her people, friends and family and such, like anyone else. All people. It was as if the world was her family and she was Mama Bear. Or maybe Mama Tiger, because it certainly wasn't a cuddly experience for anyone she perceived to be hurting someone else. It was as if, to her at least, if you stepped on one person you were stepping on all of her little cubs and tigerlings, and that wasn't okay. She made that pretty clear to anyone who belittled others in her presence, or tried to elevate themselves by pushing someone else down.

Olive Marin, childhood friend of Dr. Amelia Pope

Amelia was protective of folks when we were kids, you bet. It was a really inclusive thing, but also kind of brutal, if you ever stopped to think about it.

Here was this little girl who wasn't exactly unfriendly, but certainly not…nice. Not your first choice to have at slumber parties, you know? But she was there for you when no one else was. And not because she thought it would give her some kind of social status or whatever. I don't think she cared too much about schoolyard politics. It was more like she hated injustice and wasn't built to tolerate it. Couldn't see a wrong without trying to right it.

I remember this one time she stepped in when a pair of older boys were picking on this Latino kid at recess. We all knew these older boys' parents were a little bit racist, and so they were probably just miming what they saw at home. But this one day they shoved this kid because he looked a little different from them, and Amelia stepped right up in front of them, folded her arms, and said something like, "You realize this is making you look ridiculous?"

The boys tried to posture a bit like boys will do, but they were also looking around at each other, and at all the other kids who had gathered around since they shoved that Latino kid, and it seemed to dawn on them that they were kind of acting like jerks in front of everybody. Or maybe they just felt a little silly for being stared down by a little girl who was spindly and small and much younger, and who they clearly couldn't just shove out of the way. Not without completely losing face.

I always assumed Amelia'd either mellow or get really hurt at some point, because she was so set on her principles and refused to see reason when you'd tell her to just leave things well enough alone. We didn't really keep in touch after school, so I didn't know what she was up to. Some people get a little softer with age, and they fill the space the good Lord gives them by being a little bit flexible. That's something most people learn to accept as they get older. Amelia, though, it's almost like she became harder over time. Like the world pushing against her toughened her skin rather than the other way around. I guess we need people like that as much as the other, but I sure am glad I don't have to carry that kind of burden.

Dr. Robert Chalmers, Pediatric Psychologist

Amelia's parents first brought her in to see me when she was seven years old.

At that age, Amelia was already showing signs of character traits you don't typically see in children. Some patients develop such traits in their late-teens, but even then, very seldom.

Amelia had a level of self-awareness that was remarkable, and this helped her stand out from most of my other patients. Much of the time it was as if I was discussing philosophy with a first year college student, rather than trying to help a troubled child cope with a world in which she didn't quite fit.

I recall that during one of our visits she was incredibly frustrated by injustice and intolerance, and was having trouble comprehending how her peers could fail to see the misalignment of the world that she clearly and intensely perceived. She couldn't fathom how other people looked past that other, perhaps deeper level of human interaction. A level in which all the pieces fit together, sometimes in a beneficial way, but more often non-optimally.

Amelia would often interject on someone else's behalf, and sometimes even place herself in harm's way to make a point. She was trying to educate her peers, and even adults, about how to behave, I think.

For Amelia, day-to-day life was like listening through the ears of an impresario to a musical score containing a hint of discord: she felt compelled to tune the strings and set things right. To make the world a more perfectly orchestrated place.

Eugene Crisp, Chief Storyteller at Proxy

Dr. Pope was not a large woman. Not muscular, nor menacing. Looking at her, without context, you would see a Caucasian female of fairly unremarkable proportions and aesthetics. Sharper-than-average cheek bones cutting across a cherubic, inverted-teardrop face.

Dr. Pope's power was derived not from sinew or imposing frame, but from an understanding of what was happening around her as it happened. She grokked what other people were thinking with whipcrack speed, and simultaneously determined how other people thought she was thinking. She could unravel a tangle of intentions and perceptions, which resulted in a well-labeled subway map of facial expressions, body language, meaningful emphasis, and subjective definitions for the words being used.

Dr. Pope was remarkably attuned to the minutiae that many of us take for granted. She embraced this awareness, and after high school stepped out into the waves, far from shore, allowing the current to take her far from the small New England town where she grew up. This roil eventually deposited her, sand dollar-like, on the shores of the Pacific Northwest.

It was in Seattle that Dr. Pope initially found firm footing in the entertainment sector; video games, specifically. She liked that it was an industry in which very intelligent, creative people wove together experiences for the average person. An industry full of outliers struggling to communicate grand ideas and concepts.

It was also an industry in which, despite the grand technologies, resources, and minds involved, even the most established industry leaders seldom delivered more than me-too efforts, or in her words, "Trope-laden mind-candy." These companies churned through zillions of dollars to develop products that were unchallenging, addictive, and lacking substance. Mental junk food.

It was the video game industry's inability to communicate clearly, and their squandering of technologies which might serve humanity by enabling enhanced interaction and better mutual understanding, that led Dr. Pope to study artificial intelligence. She saw immense potential in these systems, especially when paired withand the multitudinous networks tendrilling across the planet. A.I. was a technology that, if developed and used correctly, could allow for new types of interactive media, revolutionary interfaces, and radically different platforms through which anyone with something to say could communicate more clearly.

She envisioned a world in which our online lives overlapped with our real-world lives to the point where it would be hard to distinguish one from the other. Virtual guardian angels would protect us from harm, while also helping us get the most out of our day. This would allow the aggregate wisdom of the human race to manifest as a virtual assistant of sorts, a friend customized for each and every person in the world. A faux personality that would help balance each person's imbalances, smooth over jagged social interactions, and allow us to work with each other toward common goals.

All her life, Dr. Pope had felt like a pro-athlete endlessly circling a practice track but never going full-out and expending all of her potential energy toward a worthwhile goal.

After a few years of graduate school, then a few more to achieve her doctorate in artificial intelligence, Dr. Pope took on a lead technology development role at Crytical Games in Seattle. It was there that she decided to stop running laps.

PROXY

Dr. Sunder Davies, Simulation Department Head at Proxy

Dr. Pope enjoyed the challenges inherent in working within the video game industry, but she didn't particularly like the industry itself.

For a sector predicated on technology and the advancement of the same, the video game world seldom broke molds or contributed beyond its latent value as an entertainment mechanism. Like movies and television before it, video game developers sometimes dabbled in making art and telling good stories, but all too often, and increasingly so at that point in time, the pursuit of blockbusters guided development rather than the other way around, and accountants and executives who lacked aspiration or inspiration were deciding how to best harness new developments in graphics, processing power, user interface hardware, and energy efficiency.

This wasn't news, and it wasn't the first time technologies

with so much potential were hindered by their initial, successful consumer use-case. The printing press became a big deal because it allowed publishers to print more. Bibles and make more money. It was quite some time before the value of their remarkable moveable type innovation was utilized for something less immediately sellable, but far more impactful in the long-term.

Dr. Pope thought her colleagues lacked a sense of purpose, and felt that the whole industry needed to step back and take a long look in the mirror. Rather than helping the world become a better place by allowing human beings to connect with one another and gain new perspective through interactive narrative, which is what it seemed capable of doing right then more than ever, the video game industry had gelatinized into a cesspool of passivity, misogyny, and underwhelming products.

Her co-workers were cavemen with computer science degrees. The game-playing audience, in her mind, were lost souls looking for answers and meaning. But all they were ever offered were more tits and explosions.

I didn't tell her that I enjoyed some of the games that were available during those years because I understood her larger point and didn't want her to get the wrong idea. I didn't buy them for the breasts or the bombs.

Miles Anthony, Chief Executive Officer at Crytical Games

It's weird contrasting the woman who worked for Crytical back in the day with the person I would hear about later, first for what she did in the field of robotics, then, well, everything else.

Amelia, that is, Dr. Pope, was a talented person, but she really didn't fit in too well with the Crytical culture. She was great at repurposing existing tech and helping develop new platforms and graphics engines and properties. Some of her simulation stuff? Gold. Triple-platinum, if we'd measured things that way. I mean, lots of people are involved with the development of any product, but I totally give her credit for the *Life on Earth* series. Very clever use of our Utility Engine development suite, and it helped us leap ahead of some of those other lifestyle simulation MMORPGs that were gobbling up our market share at the time.

But unfortunately, ah, well she didn't really get along with too many of her co-workers. Her superiors found her to be insubordinate pretty much all the time, and her inferiors found her to be a little aloof, even a little antisocial.

Which is fine, you know? We embrace all personality types at Crytical. Ask anyone and they'll tell you what a welcoming community we are. *WIRED* ran a piece about our colorful and approachable office environment. But even the smallest joke seemed to infuriate her and she'd get all cold and abrasive. It was irrational. And, well, Crytical is a fun company, that's just the culture. People play practical jokes on each other, drink after work, and yeah, maybe sometimes the jokes are borderline racy, but we're all adults, right? There was no need for her to be so uptight all the time is all I'm saying.

Bethany Petrah, former Executive Assistant at Crytical Games

Thank. God. For. Amelia.

Those boys were just…it was horrible. She was the only reason I was able to…well, let's just say she was a big part of why there wasn't a non-stop barrage of harassment lawsuits aimed at the Crytical top brass, and why there wasn't more alcoholism amongst the female staff members working there. It was like working in a frat house, and all the punks signing your paychecks saw it as a perk to join in on the 'fun.' Bastards.

Amelia kept those boys in line, though. As much as any group of tech-industry man-children can be brought into line, I mean.

Eugene Crisp, Chief Storyteller at Proxy

Many creative luminaries have 'into the woods' stories, during which they leave the sane, structured world behind and find themselves wandering purposeless, unsure of how to apply themselves and their efforts. In some cases it manifests as the first time they've ever lacked a goal or project.

For Dr. Pope, Crytical was a deep, dark forest, full of dragons to slay. She was one of the few female employees at that particular boys club, and her efforts to guide the company toward a more diverse portfolio of offerings were met with far less than enthusiasm.

She made partnerships with indie hardware developers, bringing them into the fold, which gave Crytical a jump-start in the budding virtual reality gaming scene. She captured the new casual-enthusiast gaming market, which encompassed multiple age demographics full of people who were engaged with gaming, but who felt ostracized by existing gamer culture. She also coined a new type of game genre: the real life simulation, or RLS. This genre made use of newly developed wearable technologies with sensors which allowed people to 'level up' by living their lives. Learning new skills was one way to gain experience, for example, and the game interfaced with online education portals that incentivized real world personal growth alongside in-game virtual growth.

Despite these successes, for the better part of three years there were subtle threats leveled, hinting at repercussions should Dr. Pope fail to toe the company line. She was a diversity metric for their portfolio; y-chromosome-lacking 'minority hire' who allowed the company to posture for the press and get away with the many ethical lapses that leaked out to the public. Harassment and mismanagement of funds were just two of many boardroom concerns at Crytical, and she was a source of positive press any time they needed to sweep some new scandal under the rug.

Dr. Pope was aware of this, and was aware that she would probably have a much easier time if she just fell into lockstep with company's continued production of the same old profitable garbage. But she never did. She never stopped pushing for broader offerings, a more welcoming corporate climate, and a more inclusive library of games optimized for a larger demographic span.

As a result of her ongoing defiance, Dr. Pope was typically overlooked when it came to promoting new blood into leadership roles, and she experienced a slow roll-back of her authority and responsibilities. The final year of her employment at Crytical was molasses-slow, as much of her work had been reassigned to someone else, one of her many peers who were willing to play ball.

Dr. Pope found herself sitting at her desk one day, thinking big thoughts before allowing them to fizzle, powerless to make any kind of impact within the entangling corporate structure of Crytical. Unable to abide an unsolved puzzle, she decided to get some perspective. The solutions to her problems would not be found within the same structure that created them, she knew, so she'd need to break her routine.

In what would later be seen as a pivotal decision, Dr. Pope decided to try something unfamiliar. She decided she would figure out how to have a social life.

Dr. Sunder Davies, Simulation Department Head at Proxy

During her time at Crytical, Dr. Pope met a guy named Anesh. I think at a game conference or in some other social-but-technically-professional setting.

He was interested in her as a potential recruit, at first. There weren't as many women involved in the video game scene back then, and that made it difficult to find qualified women to hire. At some point, however, he became interested in her personally.

For Amelia to accept an offered date was unusual. Maybe unprecedented. It's still hard for me to picture, actually, because she was incredibly focused on her career and never seemed too interested in personal matters.

The way the date turned out, though, was pure Amelia.

Anesh Dhillon, Founder and CEO of Dissipation Technologies

It was one of the stranger dates I've ever been on, and I've been on plenty. When you rise up to a certain level in any industry you get attention for it. I mean it wasn't that difficult to find company for the night. For dinner, I mean, but otherwise, too, if I'd wanted. You know what I mean.

Anyway, she was hesitant to go out until I told her what I did, at which point she told me a time and a place, just like that. I like a girl who knows what she wants, you know? I'm not threatened by that. So I said okay, and we met at this place that wasn't as fancy as I would have thought, since I was obviously picking up the bill and some women like to live that up a little, but the food was pretty good. Not much in the wine department, but it was cool. Lady's choice.

I asked her about her family and what she did for fun and all that, but she kept pulling the conversation back to work. Wanted to know about Dissipation and our goals and our next steps, so I told her what I could.

I want to make very clear that no matter what the board has claimed over the years, I did not tell Amelia anything that wasn't available in the public record. All I did was describe the Dissipation concept. We were developing a computing technology made up of distributed, networked components. I maintain that she must have figured out the rest on her own. Maybe she called in some friends to help her reverse-engineer the idea or something, I don't know.

Our approach was still better, of course. I still maintain that, it's undeniable. But she did a lot more with the concept than I would have assumed she would have been able to. I mean, just based on her background and her lack of familiarity with the technology. Not because of anything else.

At first, later, when I found out what she was up to, I was all, "Well, isn't that flattering?" You have to get used to this kind of thing, working between the Valley and the larger Silicon Coast. Lots of me-too companies popping up all over the place pretty much all the time. You get big enough, someone always wants your balls. I mean in the business sense. I'm talking about copycat entrepreneurs.

And then. Well. Amelia took our work — I mean, a similar kind of work that was maybe built based on a loose idea of what we were working on, regardless of what the board says — in a strange direction.

Our patents at DT were, and still are related to the dissipation of components throughout a fluid to reduce friction and heat. This allows you to build a server farm in a tank of water or some other heat-disseminating medium, right? So, Amelia took a different route and decided to build the first literal 'cloud computer,' instead. Completely different thing, not something we can legally act on, or something a CEO can be ousted over. You can't stop someone from having a good idea.

It's fine. I was, and am, totally fine with it. The notes from our on-record board meetings will show that I've explained as much on several occasions.

Eugene Crisp, Chief Storyteller at Proxy

Dr. Pope's interest in Mr. Dhillon was strictly professional. She was fascinated by his company's concept of breaking a processor into pieces and thought that in addition to the heat dispersal benefits that Dissipation Technologies was touting, there could be other, more structural benefits to such a system.

The big potential to Dr. Pope was in a distributed computer's modularity. One could conceivably use incredibly cheap and low-market components, and creating extensive daisy-chained webs of components, one could create an ever-scaling machine capable of sharing computational loads between its widespread components. The wireless technologies to connect the pieces existed, as did the software to manage such a system. The main hurdle was figuring out how to optimally arrange the pieces.

The standard method for building a computer has traditionally involved trays of chips and solid-state drives. These trays were hung in filing cabinet-style closets, in drawers which could be pulled out and swapped as necessary, replaced when broken or when a newer version became available.

A core issue with such a system is how to deal with energy. On two different fronts.

First, you have to power the array of components themselves, which can require a significant amount of electricity. Large tech companies with server farms dotting the planet have plugged their computers into vast fields of solar panels, enormous flower-like wind turbines, and have even loaded their components onto ships, allowing underwater turbulence and the temperature disparity in the water to power or partially power their technological infrastructure.

The second and sometimes trickier energy-related problem is that this equipment generates a great deal of heat as it operates.

This heat must be dispersed, and this dispersal can be a real headache, as the larger processor stockpiles can get so warm that they shift the microclimate of the region in which they're based. As such, server farms have been built in both arctic climates and deep underground so that the natural chill of the earth around it can deplete much of the energy radiating outward. Others have been distributed as farm nodes, which are smaller server farms linked by high-yield fiberoptic cable, the same type of cable that would connect each machine to the others if they were in the same room rather than scattered across a continent.

It seemed to Dr. Pope that if she could solve the triple-problem of heating, dispersal, and modularity, she could build something truly monumental. She could do work many magnitudes larger in scale and ambition than had been done before. She saw that Mr. Dhillon was on to something, but that he wasn't taking full advantage of what might be accomplished with the concept.

But she also wasn't certain that her analysis was sound, so after that fateful not-date, she contacted a man she'd often worked with in school.

As a functional theorist in the field of A.I., Dr. Pope was capable of handling a great deal of heavy developmental lifting when it came to software. But the hardware required to run what she had in mind would require an immense amount of customization, essentially the design and production of a system that required several novel components.

Matthew Gruber had worked as her university's on-call I.T. technician, but in his free time he was a hardware hacker for hire, with self-taught credentials and professional experience in everything from transistor refurbishing to tele-robotics.

In the years since they'd first met, Mr. Gruber had gained notoriety for his hacks and inventions, which he displayed online, along with tutorials showing how others could replicate his feats. He published these works with an Open Source license so that anyone who wanted to could riff on his work and share any improvements they innovated. He'd had several offers to host TV shows on which he'd build flame-throwers and robotic dinosaurs, or maybe compete against other gearheads for tech-enthused crowds, but he'd turned them all down. He made a decent living from his online videos and enjoyed the freedom to tinker as he pleased.

He was, however, a man who appreciated a challenge. And Dr. Pope had one she thought might lure him from his workshop.

Matthew Gruber, Chief Hardware Specialist at Proxy

I remember when Pope came to me with the cloud computer idea. It wasn't a truly original concept, and I told her as much, flat out.

Some garage geeks tried to do something similar back in the early days of solid state memory. But it hadn't really been possible before pretty much that very moment that Pope started talking about it, because the requisite components had only just arrived on the market at a price that was affordable enough to make fabrication feasible for a budget smaller than the GDP of a small European country And it was only that year that at-home micro-scale fabricators that worked with the right materials became available outside of assembly shops owned by big dog, asteroid-mining tech companies.

It's important to remember that Pope was coming at this thing from a very different angle than most people in the computing world. The players in almost every tech-related field were looking to build bigger and better server farms, so the work those jokers over at Dissipation were doing made sense on paper and attracted a whole lot of venture cash from the outset. They were building decent solutions for existing problems. They were trying to build a better box rather than thinking outside of it.

Pope, though, was interested in intelligence. Simulating life. And true artificial intelligence had never been possible because you can't actually program randomness into something. No matter how many times the developer gods of old made the attempt, trying to program something that's truly random never worked.

You can fake it, of course. And you can muddle the process with reroutes and blind paths and a whole lot of other coding magic that makes something seem random, especially to a human viewing it from the outside, one who's not watching all the sprockets spin and switches flip. But unscramble the convoluted thing and trace it back to the original code and it's all the result of human-written instructions.

That's the issue with traditional cryptography, by the way. And traditional artificial intelligence. Stare at any of them long enough, run them through the right de-scramblers, and you can see the pattern. You can see the script an 'intelligence' is acting out. Sprockets and bolts and tiny little watch parts, but still a system built to operate in a given way, following a pre-ordained path.

So Pope knew about this problem and was thinking about the dissipation of computer components and she realized that the whole industry was predicated on making computers that are more and more powerful so they can better trick the end-user more elegantly and thoroughly.

But taking that path would only ever result in interface trickery, not the actual machine intelligence she'd always wanted to achieve.

We actually tried some interesting stuff back in the day, when she was in school and I was futzing around at the university building. We met up at a casual hacker soiree, thrown by one of those kids who enjoys throwing salon-type get togethers. Pope and I probably wouldn't have met until much later, or at all, had we not been there that night. We talked, among other things, about building an upgraded version of Conway's Game of Life.

The idea of the GoL is simple: it's a script that automates cells. It was made by this guy John Horton Conway in the '70s, and all you have to do is set an initial state for the cells that are present. Those cells then replicate and move and evolve within a grid based on the rules that you established.

The variation, the seeming-randomness you can get with this game is incredible. A lot of folks who're just learning about computers will see the GoL and have their minds blown. They immediately try to figure out how to breed 'puffers' or 'gliders' or other types of creatures, though the 'creatures' here are just little square pixels on a grid, their shape and movement determined by very basic mathematical rules. It makes you appreciate real life in a different way, as something both more simple and more complex than you had imagined.

So we spent a few weeks fiddling with our own version of GoL, but eventually stepped away from it, realizing that it was a system we could make very complex, but in which we were still beholden to certain natural barriers that existed within code. We could make something that seemed very real, very random, but it was still just fancy tricks that looked real, pretended to be random. Pope refocused on video games after that, deciding that if she was going to fake real life, she might as well fake it in a compelling and realistic way. I went back to some other projects I was working on before she and I got ourselves sidetracked.

We kept in touch, off and on. I'd consult with her on hardware, she'd help me get around a roadblock with software. Through the rest of her educational career, though, and into her professional career, the thing that always frustrated Pope was that faster processors simulating intelligence meant better special effects, but everything was still fake no matter how real it seemed.

Fom our GoL experiments she knew that the way folks have been building A.I. for games was foundationally wrong. Everyone was hitting nails with bigger and bigger hammers, hoping that maybe their hammer would someday be big enough to turn their target into a screw.

When she came to me about this meeting she'd had with that Dhillon guy, she'd finally realized that she needed to just use a screw from the outset, instead. A screw accomplishes something similar to a nail, right? It's a parallel tool. But it operates in a very different way, has different physics behind it. If she wanted to build legit A.I., she'd need a new approach. Something that seemed the same to those who looked at it but operated differently underneath the surface.

That's why she came to me to help her build the Approximation Engine.

Dr. Sunder Davies, Simulation Department Head at Proxy

I wrote my dissertation on how one might economically scale virtual representations of intricate and complex systems, such as those that predict weather patterns or accurately display biological ecologies.

I grew up in Sohra, a small town in northeast India. I moved to the US when I was a child, but much of my extended family still lives in Sohra, and their problems are numerous, but most derive from their dramatic rainfall.

Sohra has several times had the distinction of receiving the most rainfall of any city on Earth, and this rainfall has eroded their soil. This has led to a strange situation in which the town with the most rainfall on the planet regularly suffers from both drought and is covered with inedible, rugged plant life. The rains are regulated by the monsoons, but global weather patterns are ever shifting, and with increasing speed and intensity. My family would survive, I knew, but they were suffering.

My educational pursuits were sparked by the desire to map these weather patterns. If I could minutely simulate the variables that conspire to create climates, could areas such as Sohra better prepare for the future? Could they be forewarned of extreme weather events, and more prepared to bulwark their landscape during times of relative calm?

Weather simulation, unfortunately, seemed to be a pariah in the field of technology. Though there were efforts to explain and display weather for internet and news program consumption, the ability to accurately predict these events on a tiny scale, a size that could benefit a particular region or city, were not forthcoming. Major advances had been made in satellite mapping and tracking, but predictive technological development was at a near standstill.

Part of the reason for this research stasis was that accurate simulations of any kind have traditionally required just as much computing power at scale as they have in micro. In other words, if it cost x to map one storm system, it would cost $10x$ to map ten of them. There were zero processing savings at scale, which was limiting on many levels, but particularly the ever-so-important monetary one.

The work I was doing had me importing the US Meteorology Department's global weather data, all of their data, and crunching it in such a way that I could reliably view trends and represent them visually in real time, from the micro up to the macro. My theory was that I could make better use of processing resources by representing data bits as particles and waves, rather than metaphorical numbers and graphics. That is to say, I wanted to rebuild reality within a computer, from the most fundamental components, the quarks and atoms, all the way up to where they become weather and land mass.

This is a stark contrast to how such simulations are usually built. Typically you go from large to small, starting with the complex system that you can easily see and represent, and then working downward to show the minuscule, but processing these microsystems the same way you'd process the larger whole. You'd build the mountain, then exert more processing power to show the individual boulders, then even more to show the moss on those boulders, and even more to show the one-cell-thickness leaves which make up the moss.

As a result, smaller, more detailed systems required even more processing power to simulate than the larger ones, and the more fundamental your simulation, the more significant the drain on your computing infrastructure. This meant that even the smallest, simplest representations of real-life systems required days of processing on rented supercomputers to accurately render. This was not practical for the types of uses I envisioned.

I wanted to flip that trend by starting at the micro and working upward, building the larger processes out of smaller ones. In my software, hurricanes were just the byproducts of miniature variations in temperature and moisture levels, as they are in real life. Raindrops were condensed particles of hydrogen and oxygen held together by covalent bonds and surface tension, in life and in my simulation. How about elements? Just subatomic star systems of elementary and composite particles.

I began my work at a very humble scale, attempting to replicate all of the weather data from one square centimeter of land in eastern Connecticut. After many iterations and sleepless nights, I was able to refine my model so that the physics in my micro-universe were compounding energy and matter operating at the subatomic level into the correct real-world events, just as with the aforementioned moisture variations becoming hurricanes.

I was only just beginning to see measurable reductions in processor cycle use at scale when I read a paper Dr. Pope had published on an artificial intelligence blog about some work she was doing. She posited that starting with virtual fundamental physics and building up from there could allow true intelligence to develop from foundational simulated materials, just as ours did in the real world. She even offered a few ideas as to how one might build such a simulation, though her ideas were limited to the broad strokes.

I checked her website, and it seemed she would be attending a software conference at my university later that month. I worked twice as hard to refine the system I was building during those next few weeks, but I still didn't have much to show when I arrived at the conference. The gains I'd made were almost as small as the processes I was replicating, and they were very difficult to visualize in any meaningful way.

At the conference, I tracked down Dr. Pope and convinced her to join me in a secluded corner away from the hubbub of business talk and networking taking place around us. I opened up my laptop and showed her my model.

She was very quiet for some time, and I mentally deflated, certain that she either didn't understand what I was showing her or was trying to come up with a tactful way to tell me it was a terrible idea. Or perhaps that it wouldn't work the way I thought it would.

Instead, she offered me a job working in R&D with her and a team she'd only just started assembling. She outlined what she had in mind, and I was just…I was blown away. I couldn't believe that someone else hadn't already attempted what it before, which tends to be the hallmark of a good idea.

Matthew Gruber, Chief Hardware Specialist at Proxy

Davies seemed like a questionable choice to me. He was really young, and you could tell he was an academically up-jumped teenager, more comfortable in class than the real world. The kid had brains for miles, but I didn't quite see where he fit in until I had the chance to check out the simulation he'd shown Pope.

As an actionable, testable measure of the hardware we were building, it was an amazing fit. Pope wanted to build a distributed, ever-growing computer, made up of a potentially infinite number of components. One that would scale in processing power as its cloud of nodes expanded.

Davies' software incrementally reduced the workload of whatever system it ran on, reducing energy use as it grew in complexity. He was only showing fractions of fractions of a percentage savings on processing power at the time, but Pope knew, and I agreed, that the tiny numbers Davies was working with could be pushed further with the type of system we wanted to build. Much further.

Pope's big ambition was to use our tech to evolve artificial life in a simulation in the same way it evolved in reality. That meant starting from scratch, and I mean scratch. Big bang and all that. Start from nothing, allow a universe to grow from a dust-strewn void, and then hope life emerges within that universe. If we were lucky, we'd end up with an evolved, fully-realized intelligence. Intellect that was artificial only in the sense that we grew it in a simulation. And it would be truly random because it evolved, rather than having been built. We'd give the universe instructions, physics and such, but any life that developed wouldn't have our fingerprints on it.

Davies was already making this happen, in a way. His beta software was replicating reality, from the teensy on up to universe-scale. We'd just have to upsize the thing and expand the scope. He was working with a little smidgeon of land, and we'd need to simulate, well, everything.

Dr. Sunder Davies, Simulation Department Head at Proxy

I didn't realize until much later that Dr. Pope was paying me out of pocket in the early days of Proxy. If I had realized it, I probably would have worked even harder to get the first iterations of my simulation software stable at scale. And maybe would have asked for a smaller paycheck.

But she never brought up things like that. Part of it was the project, I think, but I also got the impression that after I'd entered into her care, passed through the gates into her territory, I was wholly and truly under her protection.

It wasn't that she doted or anything like that, and she wasn't even the most communicative of employers, especially when it came to small-talk and niceties. But if I needed something, she had it for me immediately. She would never bat an eyelash, even when I requested resources that were expensive to procure. She'd just make sure she had the specs right and it would be there for me the next day, the next week, within a few hours, whatever was feasible.

That first year, it was just me and Dr. Pope in a little rented office. We had a separate room for our hardware, and a space down the hall where Mr. Gruber was fabricating the early versions of our custom components, but for the most part Dr. Pope and I sat at our computers and worked, communicating with each other in monosyllables, every Monday testing out the modifications we'd made over the course of the previous week.

Although it felt like ages before we reached any milestones of significance, it was only about eight months into that first year that we were able to test a tiny but fully-realized simulation using our own hardware, a small scale cloud computer called the Approximation Engine. The Engine was designed primarily by Mr. Gruber, who was the hardware maestro and geek-celebrity Dr. Pope had recruited to captain that wing of the project. The 'cloud' was a fog made up of dense moisture and processing components, the latter suspended in the former. The hardware segments, which were already microscopic, though not as small as we'd eventually get them, were wirelessly linked together to form a massive computing network.

Despite being intangible — you couldn't really see the computer, only the fog in which it was suspended — it was a significant step, and one that allowed me to build the The Yard, which was our first simulation larger than a cubic centimeter.

Matthew Gruber, Chief Hardware Specialist at Proxy

It was a tiny little thing, our Yard. Bigger than the centimeter-cubed example Davies' had used to win over Pope, but still very small.

Picture a family's backyard, like the kind you find behind those wall-to-wall, stucco-sided homes in Northern California. Now cut that in half. That was about the size of our virtual ecosystem. A few dozen feet square, probably, in total. All simulated, and accurate all the way down to the most fundamental particles.

I should note that The Yard was only named that way because of the size. In every other way, it was about as far from a person's backyard as you could get. It was a simulation of a nascent universe, sputtering to life. Spiraling and coalescing and pulsing with energy, but didn't have much more going on than that, at first.

We had fundamental particles of all flavors in there. Bosons and quarks, antileptons and neutrinos. These had 'grown' from our initial Big Bang event, which itself had manifested from a set of physics we programmed into the system. In short, it was a cool-ass version of Conway's Game of Life, but set way way way before life was a possibility.

The Yard changed in shape constantly. There weren't any boundaries, beyond those inherent in the amount of processing power produced by our Approximation Engine and the software sucking it up. So size, latency, and everything else were set by the maximum possible output of what we had available. A yard-proportioned space, but with ever-adjusting, infinitely flexible fences.

Eugene Crisp, Chief Storyteller at Proxy

Dr. Davies and Mr. Gruber pushed the limits of their Engine to test the veracity of Dr. Pope's plan to evolve life. They started with a pinpoint of matter, so small that it could barely be said to have existed. This particle exploded outward, reaching the fringe expanses of the simulated space within a fraction of a second, roiling outward with a ferocious amount of energy. It began to cool along the fringes, pulled back inward and compressed once more, then pulsed outward a second time.

It was a microcosm of the real universe, constructed using the most stable available theories about the universe's origins. Though the three-person team would later adjust and improve the math upon which the tiny universe was built, and though they would later construct a universe in which time operated at a pace similar to the rate at which we experience it, rather than radically sped up as was the case with the initial tests, and though the wonders they would see soon enough would eclipse the miniature universal explosions that were the pinnacle of their initial experiment, both Dr. Davies and Mr. Gruber would later admit to remembering that specific moment as the most beautiful and awe-worthy of their time at Proxy. To them, it represented a simple idea constructed cleverly, quickly, and for the first time.

That the simulation worked made them both wonder what they might accomplish if they put more thought, time, and resources into it.

Dr. Sunder Davies, Simulation Department Head at Proxy

Dr. Pope developed an interface that linked my simulation software with Mr. Gruber's hardware so that we could more easily observe and measure the results of that synthesis. Her efforts on this front are why we were able interact with our cloud and yard at all, in fact. An entire operating system had to be developed, and she built the bare bones of one while we were parsing the ingredients for that initial simulated Big Bang.

With her interface in place we still couldn't actually see the universe forming, but we could tell it was happening. The readouts the system generated were statistical and based on the same notational systems used in astronomy and physics. We didn't have the bandwidth to spare for displaying graphical interfaces at that point, but we could all read the notation decently well, and could recognize the beauty in what was happening in the numbers.

Eugene Crisp, Chief Storyteller at Proxy

Proxy, Inc. was registered as Dr. Pope's holding company for the simulation project. She officially founded the business the day she quit her job at Crytical Games. From there, Dr. Pope got to work finding funding for the effort.

Up until that point she'd been paying out of her own bank account. Without her job at Crytical, there was only so long she could keep the company solvent without outside resources. Registering Proxy as an official, taxable entity allowed Dr. Pope to accept investments, which she used pay her staff and cover rent.

Her initial investors were former coworkers and classmates, people who had worked with Dr. Pope and knew her potential, despite not knowing much about how she intended to generate a return on their investment. She pitched them on the hardware component, which she could demonstrate and quantify based on existing hardware companies' valuations. She mentioned their efforts with simulations, but as a secondary product. These primary investors were sold on the cloud computer concept alone.

With that seed capital, Dr. Pope moved Proxy into a larger space, which contained a machine shop, laboratory, and offices; a significant upgrade from the sub-leased office from which they had been working. She also hired four new people for the team.

Dr. Jim Walters, Physicist In Residence at Proxy

I wasn't sure about the whole dang concept from the get-go. I walked into the company offices that first day, and I tell you, I was thinking, "Darnit Jim, what did you get yourself into, here?"

But the contract I'd signed stipulated that I'd have a month to settle in and get my bearings, and if I wanted to leave I could take off, just like that, so I was willing to give it a chance. The people were friendly at least, and they all seemed to be passionate about what they were doing, and smart whips, all of them.

The project was impressive, though I didn't see where I fit in with everyone else, at first. Dr. Pope answered all of my questions early on, and she helped me understand the remarkable concept they'd been working on. It was a splendid idea, the cloud computer, though I did wonder how the heck they intended to whittle it into something practical.

On my first day at the office, they'd just finished building what's called a 'sandbox world,' and it was probably the best example I'd seen, in terms of construction. It didn't look very pretty, just a bunch of numbers and what have you, flickering across some cheap monitors, but it worked like a dickens. The numbers were mostly accurate and represented things I hadn't seen worked into simulation formulae before. As a gen-u-wine physics geek, stepping into that office was like walking into a grown-up playground.

There was a lot left to do, though, you know. Their physics, for instance, were based on outdated research. They were building a universe, but they'd never get the artificial life they were hoping for using the values they had in there. Their variables were taking them to universal heat death too quickly.

Which is why they needed a physicist on hand, I guess. The hardware was splendid, and the sandbox universe was darn cool, but there were a lot of little things that needed tweaking if they ever wanted their simulated aliens to grow inside the thing.

Joan Deacon, Chief Financial Officer at Proxy

I was ostensibly the CFO at Proxy, but I was also kind of the only real business person there. Don't get me wrong, Amelia had a sort of latent sense for the commercial side of things. But good sense will only get you so far, and she had the smarts to know when she needed to bring in bigger guns.

I think my strong relationships with many and varied venture capitalists helped my case when we had our little interview. The concept she wanted to sell was going to be a difficult pitch even if we already had something shelf-ready, and we were ages from knowing when we'd be able to develop, polish, and market a product to even a single demographic. That meant we had no idea when we'd have a business model that would put us in the black. So it would be my job in the meantime to pull in some dreamers with cash who could understand why this thing we were building was a big deal, even before it had become an obvious one.

Thankfully, I had in my contact list a few dozen aspirational-astronaut billionaires who wanted to save the world and make it a little nerdier at the same time.

Also thankfully, Amelia already had a good idea of how to leverage the artificial intelligences she was hoping to grow within the simulation. She told me, "Joan, the A.I. software on the market today will continue to get incrementally better, probably forever. But this simulated reality we're growing will allow us to evolve true intelligence, which means the A.I. we're selling as personal assistants, as smart-home monitors, as anything we can imagine, will actually be intelligent. All these other 'intelligences' are just bits of code faking consciousness. Ours will be conscious."

That really got me thinking, and I put together a killer pitch stack. I could sell the idea of investing big once in order to blow everyone else out of the water in a huge industry, maybe multiple industries, and maybe forever. That was a storyline I could sell.

Money poured in from week one. Booya.

Stephanie Baxter, Biologist In Residence at Proxy

It was one of the strangest job interviews I've ever had.

I was called in by this woman who was a friend of a friend. Or a colleague of a colleague. Something like that. I'm not much of a people person. I kind of prefer to keep to myself, in my lab, with my mantises. So those social connections that lead to work opportunities don't happen for me very often.

What happened was I walked into this very clean office and sat down. Dr. Pope was one of those women who was probably referred to as a 'woman' even when she was technically more of a 'girl.' She was in her late 20's. She certainly seemed womanly to me. She wasn't super-serious or anything. But she spoke with such confidence and clarity that anything she talked about felt like the most vital subject matter in the world.

I was a little intimidated by her, actually. She was, well, quite lovely. In the way a piece of architecture is beautiful. Aesthetically pleasing because of her practicality.

I'm going off on a tangent. The point is that she was a very attractive person. And she had this very exciting topic to discuss. A simulated environment in which life would evolve, rather than being constructed. Which to my sensibilities made plenty of sense. How could we make anything other than digital marionettes if we were building virtual creatures based on what we observed about their real life counterparts, externally? That is, if we were only seeing the results of all their biological processes, but understood little about what made them function? If a heartbeat is simulated as this thing a creature has, rather than as something that makes that creature? How could we get an accurate portrayal of life without our own bias coloring it?

What was weird about the interview was that she seemed to read my mind. She seemed to know that this is how I would feel about the topic. She explained that they were aiming to create digital life in a simulated universe. I told her that it couldn't be done. Life had infinite complexity that couldn't possibly be programmed. She said, "Exactly."

Just like that, I was hooked. I got the impression most of the interviews she held went similarly, and probably finished just as quickly. How do you argue with someone who knows about the problems she faces and who has already come up with an elegant solution?

Marcus Cho, board member and minority investor at Proxy

Through my connection with Joan, I ended up in a room with Amelia, who told me about this simulation technology they were building on top of this great hardware stack. She was giving me this big pitch, and the whole time I'm just thinking, get to the point so I can give you my money.

It was brilliant. Truly. The sort of technology that, when you hear about it, and when you're someone like me who keeps their finger on the pulse of microprocessor component industries, you can't help but berate yourself a little for not thinking of first.

But that's part of what being an investor is all about, being able to recognize brilliance in the wild and helping it grow when you find it. You spot those sparks and help stoke them into massive, billowing flames.

So she gave me this pitch and it seemed to go on for hours, and partway through I just put my hands up and said, listen, Amelia, please stop. Just tell me how much you want and let's get started.

She told me, and I'm not making this up, she said she'd only let me invest if I joined the board as a minority vote. Two things, by the way, that I never do. I only join a company's board of directors when I've had a role in the growth of that company from the beginning. Only when it's my baby, you know? And I never join as a minority vote. If I'm going to take the time to help guide a company's growth, I want to know I've got the reins.

But I looked at her face as she presented these demands and thought, holy hell, this project needs this type of leader in charge. I know what I'm capable of, but creating life? Like, growing life from nothing and everything that goes with that kind of responsibility? Taking care of it and protecting it and helping it develop?

She was the person for the job, no question in my mind.

Michael Hutchins, janitor at Proxy

I was the first non-professional-hire, if you care to call it that. That's not to say I didn't know my business, I just didn't have a piece of paper to put up on the wall saying so.

Dr. Pope, you know, she's the type of lady who collects people, like she can recognize family scattered around out there in the world and she's some kind of mama-octopus, throwin' her tentacles out around their waists to pull them in. I was working in a big ol' office building downtown, bunch of Wall Street types there, people investing in things and moving around numbers on computers. Building the future, seemed like, though I didn't really understand the specifics, myself.

The doctor, she was waiting for a meeting at one of these offices and I was working on a door that'd been jamming up and causing one of the secretaries all kinds of trouble. This poor gal, young gal, just trying to make her bosses look good while keeping their schedules and typing up their notes, and this door made her look the fool while welcoming these high-flyin' folks into the main office space. I'd finished cleaning that day and decided to give the thing a look. Didn't even notice the doctor there, though she was apparently watchin' me work at least part of the time.

The door had a sensor that looked to be a little off-center, which was causing it to stutter when it unclasped with the other door. I tightened the clasp and got it flush with the lock on the other door and gave it a try. Worked real good after that.

The doctor, she says to me, "How long have you been working here?"

Took me a second to realize she was talkin' to me. Most of these fancy people in this building, they looked right past you. Made doing my job easier, you know, so I wasn't complainin', but it made getting noticed a little off-putting.

"'Bout ten years, ma'am," I said, though I almost left out the 'ma'am', seein' as how she was probably my daughter's age.

"Any interest in changing scenery? Working someplace with a little less polish?"

I told her that I didn't know, but could be.

I'd stepped aside from the door, which was good, 'cause the little secretary opened it up right about then, and I could see her trying not to look surprised that the door worked better, though she did smile with a little more enthusiasm than usual. "Dr. Pope? Mr. Cho will see you now."

Mr. Cho was one of the boss' in that particular office.

The doctor, who's name I now knew, gave me a business card when she walked by. The secretary tried not to look surprised. The doctor said, "Let me know if you're interested. Smaller place, but there will very likely more of this kind of thing," she pointed at the door, "to handle. I'm sure we'd be able to use a man of your talents."

I smiled and nodded, not sure what to say to something like that, particularly with the secretary standing right there. I called her later, though, and asked if I could see the space.

It was a little tiny strip mall location, pretty much, though there weren't any other shops in the area, just this one space that had a tiny little lobby and a few offices and a kitchen and what looked like some kind of TV studio setup. There was a little garage area the doctor told me was their machine shop, though beyond a few power tools and some work tables there wasn't much in there, and definitely nothing you'd call a 'machine.'

The place was a mess, like she'd just moved in. The kitchen was only a kitchen because it had linoleum floors, a long table with some chairs, a fridge, and a microwave. The other rooms were the same, only called offices in the loosest way, because that's how the furniture was set up. Looked like it may have been furniture left over from the last tenant.

I asked Dr. Pope what they were doing there, what kind of business she was running out of a place like that, and I tried to say it without accidentally maybe offending her, because maybe she thought the place was a real sweet setup.

She told me that they were going to 'give birth to artificial intelligence.'

I nodded and smiled and told her that was real nice, but I was thinking in the back of my mind that maybe I shouldn't quit my job at the downtown office after all.

She told me I could work after-hours, part-time, and quoted me a respectable hourly rate. I could work both jobs if I wanted, she said, or change over to full-time whenever. I told her I could start then and there, that night, if she wanted. School payments for my daughter weren't cheap.

Eugene Crisp, Chief Storyteller at Proxy

The core team assembled, Amelia led Proxy in an inverted exploration of what was possible. Heads down, noses applied firmly and stubbornly to grindstones, the team worked, ate, and sometimes slept at the office. Social lives fizzled and outside relationships were strained, but the work was done, and the satisfaction derived from that work was immense.

Dr. Walters worked with Dr. Davies to recalibrate the numbers that determined how physics manifested in the simulated sandbox universe that had been dubbed The Yard.

Dr. Baxter worked on a roadmap of the milestones they'd need to reach for life to germinate within their lifeless soup of elements and energy. She outlined checklists that would lead to a type of life as similar to our own as possible, so that we would recognize intelligence when we saw it, and so that there would be as many potential uses for that life as possible.

Mr. Gruber furiously iterated the drives, memory, and micro-antennae that floated as particulates in the foggy body of the cloud computer. Some days he would work his way through five generations of a static-disperser or communication filament, each batch a small improvement upon the last.

Ms. Deacon honed the organizational structure of Proxy, Inc, establishing a board of directors with Dr. Pope at its head, filing patents on the cloud computing innovations and Dr. Davies' simulation software, and conducting assessments of the business landscape surrounding the major products that might emerge from the work already being done and the work that might come next.

Even Mr. Hutchins, the janitor, found that he wasn't able to spend as much time with his daughter as he would have liked, often staying at the office late into the early hours of the next day after his shift to help Mr. Gruber with the fabrication process. The man had proved to be quite a skilled hand hardware.

What goal kept the Proxy team so focused, so neglectful all other worldly duties?

Stephanie Baxter, Biologist In Residence at Proxy

Amino acids. We needed to evolve a universe that would manifest matter, which would eventually aggregate as land mass, which would then foster amino acids.

There's a chance that life can evolve in other contexts. Extremophiles of the kind we've found on Earth are a testament to how diverse even our own carbon-based lifeforms can be. But we were aiming to develop intelligences that would be useful in the real world. Our world. That meant intelligences with whom we would share common ground. Planet-based creatures. "Life as we know it," to ruin a quote by Isaac Asimov.

What we needed was another Earth, or something incredibly similar. A viable habitat in which intelligence of the kind we would recognize as such could evolve. If we were lucky, a simulated animal intelligence would gain sentience and we'd have created the first true, human-equivalent intelligence we've ever encountered beyond our own species.

Which is a heavy topic. If you think about it.

Joan Deacon, Chief Financial Officer at Proxy

Everyone made a very big deal about the 'intelligence question.' Namely, if we managed to create a universe that harbored intelligent life, would that life be, you know, alien life? Would it be foreign enough for us to learn from? Would its existence create some kind of existential crisis for humanity?

These were important questions not just for us on the team, but in terms of what we could then do with the A.I. once it was born. If focus groups were frightened by the concept of interacting with alien life, we would have to keep it on the down-low and maybe sell it as a B-to-B solution, like personal assistants that would cost nothing to operate. An enterprise solution, but not something everyone would have built into their phone.

On the other hand, if the A.I. proved to be publicly acceptable, or at least, not something that people seemed to care about too much, we could market it much more liberally. Virtual friends. Customer service. Digital researchers and problem solvers. Maybe even use them as non-player characters inside of video games.

Dr. Sunder Davies, Simulation Department Head at Proxy

We scaled a lot after the initial surge of cash came in from investors. Because Dr. Pope didn't take on enough investors to challenge her majority stake, we were able to plow through most problems without answering to anyone but her. No real bureaucracy.

Dr. Pope, as always, was driven and practical, which makes for the perfect boss, in my mind. She would ask you clarifying questions but was otherwise careful to leave you alone. She would clear all the hazards that presented themselves so you could focus on your work.

Once the hardware was sufficiently reinforced and we had a stable cloud computer system a few magnitudes more powerful than before the upgrade, the hardware itself became even less substantial than before. The facility in which it was located could easily be mistaken for some kind of abandoned gymnasium or vacant warehouse, but there was an invisible cloud of gas filling the space. Within that gas floated billions of tiny components, and each one a node that connected with and increased the capabilities of all the others.

Eugene Crisp, Chief Storyteller at Proxy

Computer super-charged and ready to test, the Proxy team modified the mathematical starting points for a new simulation, taking into account the physics and biological work that Dr. Walters and Ms. Baxter had done, optimizing for a more realistic universal expansion and one in which amino acids were most likely to form.

As the simulation ran, expansion after contraction after expansion, they adjusted the settings minutely over the next three months, churning through a multitude of variations. They saw matter take shape from pure energy, condense into planetoids, burst into nothingness, and start all over again. They saw this happen on repeat, endless creation and destruction, and each iteration something a little bit different, taking a different path than the last, tweaking this, adjusting that, evolutionary randomness showing them how many potential shapes might emerge from a single starting point.

Creation, destruction. Creation, destruction. Forever and ever. As the simulation ran, less direct attention was required. Social lives were reborn outside the office's hallowed walls. Diets were remembered and significantly improved. Relationships were rediscovered and strengthened. Mr. Hutchins, his wife, and his daughter took an extended weekend vacation.

And then…

Dr. Jim Walters, Physicist In Residence at Proxy

It was a Monday morning when I showed up to work and Amelia was just standing there, looking at one of the monitors. Nearly scared me half to death, her standing there like some kind of mannequin in a wax museum.

There hadn't been anything too interesting on those monitors for weeks, because the computer was cycling through versions of the simulation, each one a little different than the last. Each, so far, had failed to fulfill the requirements for an early universe that would produce land mass and organic molecules and, eventually, animo acids. Which could then lead to life, you know.

I didn't want to startle Amelia, but I caught a glimpse of what she was looking at on the monitors as I walked in, and I stepped up next to her and I just stood there. I couldn't take my eyes off it.

I must have dropped my darn briefcase, because she jumped and turned to face me. When Amelia saw me, she took a deep breath and gave one of her incredibly rare smiles. Rare as a triple rainbow, those smiles, and just as glorious. She only ever smiled when there was something truly wonderful happening.

Matthew Gruber, Chief Hardware Specialist at Proxy

Jim and Pope were just standing there in front of one of the monitors when I walked in that morning. I said "Hey" a few times but couldn't get their attention.

I went to see what they were looking at, and when I registered what the numbers on the screens were saying, I was dumbstruck, too. Just stood there speechless for a while, soaking in the moment.

Stephanie Baxter, Biologist In Residence at Proxy

Life.

Very basic life, at least.

We'd created a universe. Many, many universes. And we'd waited for mass to condense into stars, and eventually planetoids. Each and every time. Then algorithms selected the most ideal evolved scenarios and branched new potential paths using those as starting points, erasing the others to free up processing power.

In some of these universes that were generated, our planetoids converged into planets which orbited the stars. The scale of each simulated universe was limited, but each was ever-expanding. Thankfully, so was our hardware and software capabilities.

In one universe, on one of the planets, on a chunk of matter that was compositionally very much like an early Earth, they were born.

Dr. Pope tapped the monitor, startling everybody. "I need to get the graphics capabilities of the user interface up and running." She smiled. I don't think I'd ever seen her smile until that moment. It made her even more stunning.

She looked at me and said, "I want to see what our babies look like."

FIRE

Joan Deacon, Chief Financial Officer at Proxy

We didn't have a definite product in mind, not at first. We had a lot of ideas, of course, things we might do if such-and-such went a certain way. But we couldn't say for sure what would come out the other end of the simulation, you know?

One major concern of mine was that we'd find ourselves without any kind of A.I., or anything that even looked like A.I., or something that was far inferior to existing A.I. in every way. The market was saturated with clunky 'assistants' of all kinds, and though some of them were decent at enabling hands-free interactivity with devices, none of them were at all revolutionary or industry-defining. I was worried that we'd find ourselves in that same place, with just another me-too, British-voiced clickless computer mouse to show for all our efforts. A bland result like that would put us back at square one, after having spent all that money on a dead-end development pipeline.

We did have one ace in the hole, though, and that was the technology behind the simulation. The Approximation Engine, the cloud computer that Matthew built, could be used for a variety of practical purposes, and the simulation software Sunder had developed could be sold the same way, maybe even as the weather prediction app he'd initially envisioned. We could help other companies build their own, better digital worlds, and white label what we'd developed for anyone to use for whatever they were already doing. It wasn't 'the dream' the Proxy team was aiming for, but it was a way out in case everything else went to hell.

After we detected that first heartbeat, though, things were looking pretty good in Proxy-land.

Stephanie Baxter, Biologist In Residence at Proxy

There wasn't an actual, literal heartbeat. There wasn't even a heart. Or any other organ. Not at first.

What we had were cells. Cells that reproduced. We had a parallel to early Earth-life.

We'd considered the possibility of virtual panspermia. Meaning we would pepper the surface of some of the planetoids that had formed in our simulated universe with organic molecules. Maybe even fully formed proteins. To help speed things along.

This was a very distant plan B, though, because it would have run counter to our plans for evolving simulated life to begin with. We didn't want to build fake life, we wanted to let life evolve on its own.

The first iteration of molecules failed to form protocells and never achieved metabolism. Alongside the numerical interface that told us what was happening inside the simulation, Dr. Pope had set up a system that would cache a 'state' of the simulation. Which meant we could save the universe like a video game and return to that point again whenever we wanted.

The universe developed randomly based on potential paths from a given set of rules. So each time we would reset the simulator from a saved state, we'd get a different outcome. A few thousand years after a reset, which took only seconds in real-time if we sped things up, we'd have completely different results.

It took a few million automated rewindings to develop metabolism. Which sounds like a lot, but really isn't. We'd saved a cache, so it was actually kind of easy. It took few million more resets from the new, metabolism-having saved state before we began to see signs of homeostasis, structural organization, and reproduction with an error rate below the sustainability threshold. That meant our virtual life wouldn't just die out after a single generation, it would propagate, perpetuate, and evolve over time.

Michael Hutchins, janitor at Proxy

The whole office was bubblin' over about something they'd done, and I wasn't really involved with all that, but I felt excited too.

I'd started working day-shifts just a week after coming in and first seeing the place with Dr. Pope. I guess her money'd come through from the investors over at the downtown office, and it looked like they'd need some help getting some equipment set up, and then keeping it maintained for the long-haul. Some of this stuff would be getting a lot of use because it was on all the time and never shut down, so she was hoping I'd come on as a full employee of Proxy to help with that.

The hours were about the same as at the other place, but she offered me more money, which sounded just fine. I accepted and called up my manager at the other place, told him I'd found another job. He didn't seem to care too much, and had to be reminded of who I was and which building I worked in.

The people at Proxy were friendly enough, when you caught them away from their work. Like the doctor, they were the thoughtful kind, heads in the clouds, stumblin' over things as they walked to the kitchen for coffee.

Dr. Pope had her own office with its own closing door. The other people worked in shared space, with their laptop computers opened up on those tables and desks that were already in here when they moved in. I thought that maybe they'd be offended at this, all these people who were clearly doctor-types, having to bump-elbows with each other, not being shown the respect they're probably used to getting. But they all seemed pretty okay with it. I don't know if it's because of how focused they all were, maybe not even noticing the other people in their shared rooms. Maybe it was how they were divided up, with Mr. Gruber and his mile-a-minute mouth over in the machine shop, visited here and there by Dr. Davies, who seemed like a real good listener, while Dr. Baxter, who was more of a quiet-type lab doctor shared an office with Dr. Walters, who wasn't at the office very often.

Miss Deacon was some kind of business Wonder Woman,

and she spent most of her time out having meetings, which was probably for the best, seein' as how she tore the place up like a whirlwind when she stopped by to chat with Dr. Pope. Real chatterbox that gal, though I'm guessing that helped her do her job, talking so fast and furious. The higher-ups over at the office downtown were the same way.

There was a new guy who came in after I'd been working there a few weeks. He spoke with some kind of accent, though he wasn't British or anything, just a real clear talker. Dr. Pope told us that he'd be working with us, helping tell the story of the company and documenting what went on there. I hoped I'd get the chance to talk with him sometime because Dr. Pope said he was a writer. Back in the day I'd written a little bit, and I thought maybe he'd give me some pointers.

Eugene Crisp, Chief Storyteller at Proxy

It was during this span of time that I was added to the team. There was a great deal of collective anxiety at the office about communicating the importance of this technology and its potential to the world. Ms. Deacon believed that blending an author into the batter would bring the most palatable results.

Mr. Gruber and Dr. Davies were both avid science fiction readers, and were familiar with the work I'd done with NASA and the ESA in the past. After achieving some small notoriety as the author of my *Mendel's Children* series, those two space agencies had hired me to write a fiction series exploring the complexities of space exploration, the colonization of other planets, the mining of asteroids, and myriad other projects they were working on or hoping to acquire the funds to pursue. My job was to explain the importance of their work through fiction, through stories, in a way that press releases and science homework could not. These stories were then propagated as books, graphic novels, films, and television series.

Ms. Deacon believed the same could be achieved with the Approximation Engine and its resultant artificial intelligences. She hoped that I might prime humanity's collective consciousness for such a leap, so that when the technology itself arrived in the public view, it wouldn't seem like such a foreign concept. Wouldn't be perceived as threatening, but rather as a tool that would enable some wondrous things that we as a species have been dreaming of for generations — automated everything, artificial pets or lovers, all-knowing, always-on virtual assistants, machines that answered questions we didn't know to ask. The possibilities were countless and marvelous.

When I arrived at the office, the Proxy team members were analyzing something they'd created after a great deal of time and focus: rudimentary artificial life.

It's important to note before diving into what happened next that no one at Proxy had managed to get in a full night's sleep for weeks, glued as they were to their screens and interfaces. Even Ms. Deacon, who was by far the most extroverted member of the group, hadn't scheduled meetings or meals unrelate to the project within that time period.

We were either at the office focused and intense, or collapsed in a heap in our beds for a few hours. There had been no time for anything else. Regardless, everyone was feeling quite gung-ho, and this levity, combined with our intense exhaustion, resulted in some cracks.

Dr. Jim Walters, Physicist In Residence at Proxy

We were tired, oh yeah. I wanted sleep so bad that I was dreaming of it while wide awake. Lots of droopy eyelids in the office, let me tell you.

But nobody wanted to go home. There had been a wave of relief after weeks of worry. I think we were all half-afraid that the whole dang thing would just blow up in our faces. Not dramatically, not that it would actually blow up. We were worried that we'd work hard on something only to have it turn out to be nothing. A dead end. That we'd have the machines cycle through hundreds of millions of versions of our universe, and maybe tinker with the physics more, try out some of the theories that were less supported by data but which hadn't been fully disproven, but would still end up with nothing. Our little universe would remain just a fascinating simulation of nonorganic compounds. Lifeless for all simulated eternity.

Stephanie Baxter, Biologist In Residence at Proxy

The emergence of life in the simulation pulled us together as a team for the first time.

We'd been in that office together for a while. Pleasantries had been exchanged. We went through the motions. No one had put any effort into actually getting to know each other, though. No one had gone beyond hellos.

After we saw the vital signs, though, after we had metabolism, it was different. Real smiles on all our faces. Slaps on backs. People making plans for life outside the office, after things had been stabilized. Inviting each other to meet significant others.

It was like we'd witnessed a miracle only to have it taken away.

Matthew Gruber, Chief Hardware Specialist at Proxy

A reboot. We had to do a complete reboot.

It wasn't pretty, but it was necessary. And it was necessary because we'd all become so damn focused on getting the big picture right that we missed a silly detail. We failed to produce intelligent life because we didn't ensure that phosphate came into existence during the immediate aftermath of the creation of the universe.

And yes, I'm fully aware that this is something no one, except maybe some god somewhere, has ever had to say in the history of existence.

Stephanie Baxter, Biologist In Residence at Proxy

It sounds like a tiny detail, but phosphate is vital to the development of key RNA molecules.

Without proper amounts of phosphorus and oxygen scattered throughout our universe, our simulated physics wouldn't crunch them into the tetrahedral arrangement that results in phosphate. Without phosphate present to act as a catalyst, life of the kind we'd recognize wouldn't develop. Life of some sort could arise. Even intelligence could evolve, somehow.

Maybe. But it wouldn't develop in the same way it did in reality, on Earth. So if conscious, sentient life managed to evolve, we'd probably have little in common with it, if we even recognized it in the first place. Which would be interesting, but not relevant to our project goals.

Starting as far back in time as we did, every little detail was vital. Forgetting phosphate was a big detail. Really big. I was prepared to leave the project over it, because as the Biologist In Residence I should have noticed the issue early on, before we spent months coaxing our early life into existence. But Dr. Pope wouldn't let me leave.

We discussed our options and determined that a universe without phosphate was a path without a finish line. Dr. Pope killed the simulation without hesitation.

I don't mean she ordered it killed. She shut it down herself. She walked out of the conference room and into the main lab. The rest of us jumped up and followed her. She punched in her 'god mode' access password at the main terminal and had her biometrics scanned to authenticate. Then she did it. With a push of a button, our universe was gone. Just like that.

Matthew Gruber, Chief Hardware Specialist at Proxy

One moment it was there, the next it wasn't. If our simulation had been programmed into software in the traditional sense, there would have been files to delete, and the virtual-verse would have staggered out of existence, piece by piece.

Because of the nature of the hardware/software relationship in the Approximation Engine, though, our universe was essentially just a concept that existed atop our generated physics, so it was a step removed from the software. That is to say, we built the rules that built the stuff, we didn't build the stuff itself.

So when she killed the simulation, she killed physics in the simulated space, which in turn unmade the simulated reality. The universe brought into being by these rules ceased to exist.

What a way to go.

Dr. Sunder Davies, Simulation Department Head at Proxy

It would be the biggest understatement of human history to say that Dr. Pope was upset. We were all upset to the point of being catatonic.

That said, the dramatic shut-down was only dramatic because we were all aware of what had happened, and how much work had gone into it. The process itself wasn't steeped with emotion. From the moment she'd made the decision to kill the simulation and left the room, Dr. Pope seemed calm. Resolute. The drama was only implied, she added nothing negative to the mix. Something had gone wrong under her watch, and she made a difficult decision that had needed to be made. With the smallest amount of pain possible, she'd pulled off the Band-Aid.

After the deed was done, Dr. Pope came back into the conference room, gave us all some, ah, advice, and told us to take a week off.

Joan Deacon, Chief Financial Officer at Proxy

She said, "Everyone, go get laid."

I'm not even kidding. That was her advice. Then she walked out the door, got in her car, and drove away.

I texted a friend I see for drinks sometimes and told him that I needed his help with work.

Eugene Crisp, Chief Storyteller at Proxy

Dr. Pope's inspiring words in mind, we all went our separate ways. There had been little interaction between team members outside of the office previously, and that was the case in this instance, as well. Until the night before we were to return to the office.

Mr. Gruber had been talking to Dr. Davies about a graphic novel series they had both read, and they decided to continue their chat over a drink. They chanced upon Ms. Deacon at the bar, and after a round and a failed attempt to talk about anything except the office, they invited the rest of the team out, as well.

Everyone except Dr. Pope showed up over the course of the next few hours. She responded to the text saying that her night was spoken for, but that they should have a good time, on Proxy's dime.

Scientific war stories were swapped, office gossip was exchanged. There were smiles all around, and it seemed that everyone enjoyed themselves. I certainly did. Our final cheers of the night was to Dr. Pope, who was an invisible presence in the room. A woman who was as much an idea as a personality, holding the project together and bringing us, as a team, together to do something important.

We returned to the office the next day, some fortunate few having acted on Dr. Pope's advice, while others like myself mostly spent our free time catching up on our pop culture intake, sleeping normal hours, and doing as little real work as possible. We were all extra motivated to do better with the next iteration of the simulation. It was humiliating to the extreme to have spent so long building something grand, only to have to pull it apart and try again from scratch.

Everyone except Dr. Pope had arrived at the office, and since she sometimes took the punctuality-challenged local bus into work when she had a problem to think through, we knew it could be a little while before she arrived. We congregated in the conference room, reminiscing about the night before and waiting for her to show up so we could get our marching orders and get back to business.

Dr. Pope surprised us by entering the through the laboratory rather than through the lobby doors. She said, "We're back," then walked into her office and closed the door.

Mr. Gruber jumped from his seat and hurled himself through the laboratory door, emitting a loud whooping sound a moment later. He leaned back through the door leading into the conference room, a big smile on his face, and said, "She's got it back up." Shaking his head, he added, "And we've got phosphate."

Matthew Gruber, Chief Hardware Specialist at Proxy

I hassled Amelia a bit, trying to get her to spill how she'd made it happen. I figured she'd looped back around to one of our older caches, but if that was the case, I wanted to know which one.

Eventually she gave in and told me that she'd started from scratch. It took her millions of iterations at each milestone, which necessitated that she stay at the office the entire week, but she did it. She got us back on track. She rebuilt the whole damn thing herself.

That woman.

Stephanie Baxter, Biologist In Residence at Proxy

The grunt-work we were expecting to have to slog through a second time was finished. By our boss. Which meant we were able to focus on helping our replicating cellular lifeforms survive through some of the more critical moments in the evolutionary process.

We'd already moved past the stage in which our creations would replicate without being 'alive,' like viruses and other non-cellular lifeforms. What we lacked were the organized chromosomes that would store genetic materials, which are found in all eukaryotes, a family of life made up of complex organisms like plants, animals, and fungi. Without this organization, we risked walking the path of prokaryotes. Bacteria and archaea are the two best known examples from that branch of life. That would be a dead-end, and was not where we wanted to go.

Sometimes our evolutions swerved the way we'd hoped without any adjustments on our part. We assumed this meant that those turns were more likely in the real universe. In other cases it took millions of iterations before the evolutionary process went the way we wanted it to go. The leap from reproducing asexually to reproducing sexually took months, real world time.

Seeing these evolutionary sidetracks occur made me appreciate just how unlikely life as we know it actually is. But then, the fact that we could reproduce these steps after a sufficient number of attempts also implied that intelligent, carbon-based life was destined to happen countless times, in countless places throughout the universe.

Matthew Gruber, Chief Hardware Specialist at Proxy

So we had this universe, which was sprawling wider and wider, as universes tend to do. Within that universe, we had uncountable galaxies. These galaxies contained millions of stars, and those stars had chunks of mass orbiting them. Some of these chunks became planets with active geological systems, some remained lifeless balls of elemental material.

We focused on the planets, particularly the ones that developed similar attributes to Earth.

Even faux universes are too vast to easily explore, so we created filters that allowed us to find and zoom in on planets that suited our needs. After a few days of searching, we found about a dozen that were very Earth-like, down to the proportions of gases in the atmosphere. About half of those had life that was similar to early life on Earth.

We eventually decided to home in on a planet we were calling Aurora, named by me and Davies after a planet from a classic sci-fi novel. We were able to reduce our processor load significantly by re-centering our rendering mechanisms on the chunk of the universe that would most directly impact this particular planet — the planet's solar system and nearby asteroid clouds, but not much beyond that — which was an important decision because even though we had this super-powerful cloud computing setup, simulation and display at this level still churned through our processing resources like crazy.

We also decided it was time to upgrade our visualizations, which at that point were still just black and white mathematical readouts, though Pope had generated a few images of our artificial life once she got their metabolization stabilized. A consistent visual interface would allow the less statistical among us to see what was going on with graphics similar to what you might find in a video game, however. They'd wouldn't be perfectly life-like, but would be realistic enough for our purposes.

Our focal area wasn't small. We were live-processing the entirety of Aurora's home solar system, which contained three other planets, seven moons, and a central star, which was a yellow dwarf like ours. But this region was just a fragment of a mote of a speck of a pinpoint of what was going on around it. The rest of the universe was still being processed as numbers and probabilities, which would sometimes impact our small galactic neighborhood.

Focusing on this single solar system allowed us to visually render the areas we cared most about more granularly, however. We took a look at the bigger-picture when it, say, hurled an asteroid into our planet's neighborhood, but otherwise we were primarily interested in the happenings of Aurora and its two small moons.

Stephanie Baxter, Biologist In Residence at Proxy

For a period of probably five or six months in real world time, everyone's attention shifted to their individual responsibilities. Matthew on expanding and iterating the cloud computer components. Sunder on ensuring the simulation was stable and pairing well with the hardware. Jim was making sure that the physics on Aurora were matching ours on Earth, while Joan revised our financials to show the impact of our newly reduced processing costs. Eugene was being Eugene, watching everyone, asking questions. He was writing a series of short stories, I believe, about cloud computing and exponential processors. Also one about 'playing god' by creating life within a computer. It was hard to keep up, because I was busy documenting the growth of our multicellular babies.

Dr. Pope kept us all on track. Her work primarily consisted of stepping in as soon as we thought we had everyone under control and showing us that this wasn't the case. Which was good. She caught things that we didn't. Kept the big picture in mind, while the rest of us were focused on our own little facets. Having her check in on you meant you'd have a lot more work soon, something to fix or rethink, but it also meant you would be even more proud of what you'd done once you closed the gap she'd pointed out.

The initial bloom of life on Aurora was special. It

represented a real milestone. But unless you're a biologist there's not really much to see. Not much to get excited about in charting the development of a complex circulatory system. No confetti on the day you observe increased competition in pre-mammalian habitats.

Our Aurora organism forked and replicated. Over millions of simulated years it expanded into a menagerie of species. It began on the surface of the planet's warm oceans, then washed up onto land.

The organisms were competing. Changing shape rapidly. Well, rapidly in the context of biological evolution. They evolved defenses and weapons. Harder cellular shells. The ability to inject their DNA into competitors, hijacking their offspring. More potent chemical sheathes, which eventually allowed for the digestion of smaller competitors.

Some organisms evolved a type of photosynthesis, like their Earthly cousins who long ago evolved into something like modern day plankton, floating through the water, dominating the upper-ocean ecosystem with their ability to quickly reproduce and feed themselves on photons from the sun. Next, creatures capable of ingesting these pseudo-plankton became dominant.

The gas ratio in the Auroran air stayed fairly steady throughout the planet's history, but soon the plankton and their land-based siblings began to convert the non-life-sustaining toxins in the air into life-promoting oxygen and nitrogen. Just as here on Earth, each generation of life paved the way for the next generation by converting the planet into something a little different than before.

Hundreds of millions of years had passed, which was half a

year in real world, Earth time. After a long week of crossed-fingers and murmured prayers to an assortment of gods, a fragile species became less fragile, surviving when we thought it might die.

This was a creature very similar to Earth's *lystrosaurus*, and it made my corner of the lab the most popular hangout in the Proxy office.

Matthew Gruber, Chief Hardware Specialist at Proxy

It was a pig-lizard thing! Everything about it screamed digital pet.

Don't get me wrong, it was interesting in an 'early computer screen saver' kind of way when Stephanie showed me some of the fish-like creatures that were evolving in the oceans of Aurora. She showed me some crustacean-ish animals and tiny cephalopods-esque thingers, too. I was very impressed when a bunch of little pre-reptiles started to emerge from the oceans, popping their little heads up above the water. They were like a flock of tiny almost-dinosaurs, swimming around, munching on the plants and smaller beasties.

But the pig-lizard was really something special. I mean, economically? As part of some kind of virtual world business model? People would definitely pay for pig-lizards.

Joan Deacon, Chief Financial Officer at Proxy

Amelia warned us not to get too attached to the 'interim life' that evolved on Aurora because we'd be flying right by them to someplace further along the timeline. We were slowing down at certain points only to ensure that evolution was progressing along a path that mimicked the real world's developmental footsteps as closely as possible.

But these little pig dinosaur things were gold. Pure gold.

I knew we had a cache saved at that moment in time, so we could return to that period whenever we liked and copy them into massively multiplayer digital-pet-rearing video games forever and ever, if we wanted. Part of me, though, worried that we might be wasting our time going any further. There was definite value in something so cute and realistic. Something that acted so much like a real animal, because, well, it was. Kind of. Fake but real. Simulated life.

So why not quit while we were ahead? Spend what we had in the bank on reinforcing these little guys, productizing them, and trying to make something more human-like later on?

Dr. Sunder Davies, Simulation Department Head at Proxy

They were really more like large hamsters. Though they had beaks and tottered around like chunky alligators. I could see how some people would consider them cute. Like a pug or some other breed of purse-dog. It was so ugly it was borderline adorable.

Matthew jokingly called it a 'Baxtersaurus,' and the name stuck. I thought Stephanie might be offended, since the little guys were…stout. Not exactly elegant. But she seemed to love the name, and even changed the file on the creature to include the moniker.

Stephanie Baxter, Biologist In Residence at Proxy

The Baxtersaurus was similar in some ways to our planet's *lystrosaurus*, but different in many other ways. Some of the differences were substantial. Worryingly so.

The creature's brain structure, for instance, had a far more compact arrangement than than those of our higher-order creatures, with a lot less room allotted for initialized grey matter, which meant less room for iterative evolutionary changes down the line. On Earth, we humans have plenty of so-called 'junk DNA' so that the possibility of beneficial mutations arising out of seemingly nowhere is high. This junk can result in valuable evolutionary traits, though the downside is that we also have an high occurrence of non-beneficial mutations, like cancers and antisocial psychological variances. We also have excess brain matter available to take over if some portion is damaged, and we have the ability to mentally 'grow' over time in many different ways, because our additional brain space augments the latent elasticity of the organ. The Baxtersauruses lacked this excess, and as such, probably lacked our mental malleability, as well.

It also breathed differently. Due probably to the chemical composition of Aurora's atmosphere, its capillaries were a little larger, the efficiency of its cardiovascular system a little higher. Its nostril were located on its chest, which reduced the distance between its inhalation orifices and its lungs, and presumably helped it more efficiently process the not-quite-Earthly gases it was breathing.

It did seem adaptive enough to continue evolving, however, and was a close enough parallel to our own planet's early life that it wasn't prudent to reset the simulation just yet. After I'd given the Baxtersaurus a thorough analysis, I gave the go-ahead to speed the simulation back up, increasing the rate of time inside the universe back to one-thousand times faster than in the real world.

That same Earth day, a software trip-wire we'd set up was triggered. Brain capacity and structure consistent with consciousness had been evolved on Aurora. Something down there, in the simulation, on our chosen planet, was thinking. Thinking like humans.

Eugene Crisp, Chief Storyteller at Proxy

Fortunately for those of us without a PhD, Dr. Pope had upgraded the graphics on the simulation interface so that they were similar to what you could expect from studio-produced video games being sold at the time. Which is to say they were nearly photorealistic when they weren't completely indistinguishable from actual video.

The technology behind this upgrade was itself quite an accomplishment. The data being processed were not wireframes, as they would be in a video game or for special effects in a film. They were particles and photons and waves.

The Approximation Engine's efforts were displayed for us in the same way reality was displayed, by interpreting these components and processing them like the visual cortex of a brain.

In short, the interface used the same processing mechanism we use every day in the real world. The only difference was that the Engine's efforts were processed by machines and presented on monitors, while the real world is both compiled and projected inside our brains.

Dr. Sunder Davies, Simulation Department Head at Proxy

When we zoomed in to the consciousness that the Engine's filter had found for us, what we saw was a bird. Well, a bird-like creature. It was one of a small group of almost-birds living on a remote island, one of few bits of land beyond the main, single, central continent on Aurora. We watched the creature display an understanding of cause-and-effect and basic tool usage. It was sharpening a piece of a plant it had pulled off a larger stem, and was using the pointy end to pierce the soft underbelly of what looked like a tiny crab with a scorpion's tail. The extra length granted by the tool when held in the bird's toothy beak allowed it to kill and eat the crab-scorpion without being stabbed by the tail.

The variety of life that had evolved on Aurora since the time of the Baxtersaurus was astounding. There was a time, not long before in real life time, when all we had were globules of matter that Stephanie told us were alive. It didn't take long, though, before our little pet, the giant hamster beast, or rather its descendants, were just one of many types of flora and fauna on our virtual planet. Not all of these creatures were charming like the hamster-lizard, but this bird thing was quickly winning us over.

Joan Deacon, Chief Financial Officer at Proxy

It was huge. Not the bird. The bird was kind of normal-sized. For a large bird, anyway. But what the bird represented? Huge.

One of the main applications of A.I. at the time was problem-solving and computation. And you have to understand that these so-called intelligences being sold by other companies were essentially just really fast punch-card algorithms with personality overlays.

Now think about what we could do with an intelligence that was artificial, but grown or bred more like an animal. Something that actually evolved to solve problems, but didn't take up physical space in the real world the way a human or animal made of matter would.

The bird wasn't doing anything groundbreaking by modern standards. It was using a simple tool to avoid being stabbed by a crab-scorpion. But the implication was that these creatures could do way more than amble around and look cute, like the pig-dino Baxtersaurus. They possessed actual intelligence. And that I could sell.

Dr. Sunder Davies, Simulation Department Head at Proxy

The tool-using bird was remarkable. But it still paled in comparison to what Matthew called our *2001: Space Odyssey* moment.

Joan Deacon, Chief Financial Officer at Proxy

So I guess there was a movie where at the beginning a group of cavemen found a black statue. And the statue gave them intelligence. They used that intelligence to make weapons, and used those weapons to beat the hell out of a rival group of cavemen.

I told Matthew I'd watch it with him at some point, but I never got around to it.

Matthew Gruber, Chief Hardware Specialist at Proxy

Okay, first of all, it was a book that was turned into a movie.

Second, it was a monolith, planted on Earth by extraterrestrial intelligences so that…you know what? It doesn't matter.

What I meant by making the comparison was that we were able to see how such a thing might have really happened here on Earth, in real life. After the bird with its tools, we slowed down to 100 times Earth-speed inside the simulation, which allowed us to keep better tabs on some different promising species that were evolving fast and beginning to use tools.

We watched a group of primordial quadrupeds as they came down from these giant tree-like bushes they had all over the place, and tracked them as they started walking upright. Became bipedal.

We saw these new bipeds chip away at rocks, using their front-paws as hands, and gathered around the monitors to watch as they begin to use tools to lever open melon-like fruits that were abundant in their ecosystem, rather than smashing the husks. They began to use these husks as bowls to store water. We saw them use their sharp stone tools to tear sinew from bone when they found a dead animal they could eat.

We saw fire. We weren't certain if it was the first instance of intentional man-made fire on Aurora, because there were many groups at the time, and a lot of them had recognized that when they hit this rock with this other rock, they got sparks, and sometimes those sparks would cause their woven clothing and sacks to smolder. Amelia's filtering software picked up chemical shifts in the environment where fire was present, but in some cases the pings were the result of a lightning strike, and in others it was an accidental blaze caused by the sharpening of stones. So it was tricky to determine which of the individuals within these disparate groups might have been first to Prometheus' prize.

We weren't giving out trophies, though, so it was all academic. The important thing was that the rise of these fire-wielding almost-humans necessitated a change in the way we viewed our simulation and the creatures inside it.

Eugene Crisp, Chief Storyteller at Proxy

Life imitates art, just as art imitates life.

I'm reminded of this every time I hear about a new innovation that was actually invented decades before, portrayed in science fiction or on television. *Star Trek* alone is credited with inspiring hundreds of inventions and discoveries, not to mention the philosophical and social influence it had on the world.

The point is that we've been down some of these roads before, the ones we discover when we open doors that were previously closed. We've explored space, we've traveled through time, we've crossed into alternate dimensions, we've destroyed and rebuilt the planet more times than anyone can remember. The lessons are all there, approached and revisited through the eyes of the thousands of human protagonists who have explored the moral consequences and costs of anything we might someday do.

Every action has an equal and opposite reaction, and the more impactful an invention, a discovery, a groundbreaking innovation, the more dramatic the repercussions.

Joan Deacon, Chief Financial Officer, at Proxy

I think Sunder was the first of us to mention, out loud, the existential crisis he was dealing with. We were all mulling things over a little, though. Maybe different things and in different ways, but it was obvious that what we were working on was a little bigger than just the invention of some new app or gadget.

So, Sunder walked into the lab one day, during the weeks in which we were tracking these increasingly humanesque creatures. He was a little late. He looked like he'd just come out of a daze, like he'd been in a car accident or something. He didn't say hi, didn't set down his bag. He just walked into the kitchen where most of us were standing around, sipping at coffee, and he started monologuing.

Sunder said that he was concerned that we might be doing something we would regret. That creating a species for the purpose of enslavement, potential enslavement, at least, was theoretically even worse than enslaving those captured during war or stolen from their homeland. He said it was monstrous, if you stopped to think about it.

He didn't seem sure of any of the arguments he was making. It was more like he was thinking out loud and hoping for feedback. None of his words had much inflection. It was weird.

Dr. Sunder Davies, Simulation Department Head at Proxy

I remember that day very clearly. I was thinking about a redundancy I wanted to build into the simulation caching system during my commute to the office, and as I pulled into my parking spot, it all kind of hit me at once.

How was what we were doing different than, say, growing test tube babies and rearing them as slaves? How was it different than putting a bunch of sentient animals in a zoo and then breeding them for lives in captivity, for nothing more than our own amusement? Keeping animals that could think and reason as prisoners, puppets to our whims seemed wrong on so many levels.

The thought hit me like a gong mallet, and I pulled myself from my car, intending to get to work so I could put those thoughts aside until later, until I could really think them through. But it didn't work.

I think I rushed my explanation and maybe weirded everyone out. But we had a very serious talk about it over lunch that same day. Dr. Pope gathered us all in the kitchen, ordered some sandwiches, and presented her perspective on the issue.

Stephanie Baxter, Biologist In Residence at Proxy

As usual, Dr. Pope seemed to have things in hand.

She said, "What we're doing is untried territory, and we will make mistakes."

She also said, "But that doesn't mean we can't do our best to avoid the more predictable of these mistakes before we make them."

Dr. Pope said that we would avoid establishing any concrete business models until we were certain we understood what we had made. It was a new field, a new approach, and a new technology. We couldn't be certain what ethics might apply.

Thankfully, the business had been structured in such a way that she had control over Proxy's product pipeline, and the savings in processing costs because of Matthew's continued iterations in the cloud computer meant that we had money to sustain us for a while. We could afford to take the time to step carefully.

Joan Deacon, Chief Financial Officer at Proxy

I wasn't thrilled about Amelia's position, but I understood it.

I mean, it was kind of like landing in some foreign land, right? And we didn't want to be the simulated universe equivalent of the colonial empires, who raped and pillaged and took advantage of everyone they met. We didn't want to assume anything, was what she was getting at. Which made sense.

And frankly, it didn't stop me from working on potential business models, it just meant we wouldn't execute any of them until we knew enough to know what we didn't know.

Matthew Gruber, Chief Hardware Specialist at Proxy

After sharing her thoughts about what we'd do and what we wouldn't do, Amelia told us something that was just pure Amelia Pope. She said she'd be going into the simulation. Would walk around and interact. Would play it like a video game.

She'd be as unobtrusive as possible, but she wanted to 'meet' one of the simulated humanoid intelligences in their own world to get a sense of their perspective. To see their environment, their universe, as they saw it.

She wanted to understand what they thought about the world. To see if they thought to begin with.

All we knew was that there were these simulated lifeforms wandering around a simulated planet that evolved within a physics-based software sandbox. Beyond that, we were guessing. Maybe these creatures were just really good at pretending to be intelligent, but were actually no better than the AIs that were already on the market. It was hard to say from a God's-eye-view.

Of course, they could also have been as real as you or me. Simulated life, sure. But when you get down to it, all else being equal, does it matter if your reality is based on real or simulated physics? Weren't they essentially the same thing, just rules shaping a system inhabited by consciousness perceiving those rules?

Amelia wanted to figure out firsthand whether these creatures should be treated not just as virtual life, but as life.

GOD

Eugene Crisp, Chief Storyteller at Proxy

Dr. Pope called upon her experience within the video game industry to develop the virtual reality garb she wore to interact with the simulated universe. She downloaded a standard, printable goggle-and-glove architecture, had Mr. Gruber customize some of the components for her size and texture preferences, and while they were printing the polymer scaffoldings she wrote the software that would create a tunnel between her simulation operating system and the VR graphic interface.

The end result was a system that, when worn, made Dr. Pope look like she was entangled and being devoured by a robotic squid. Many of the components were wireless by default, but corded versions caused fewer latency issues and were easier to customize. They also reduced the number of software conflicts we might encounter, so each piece of the VR outfit had a thin, black cable which plugged into a control panel, which itself looked like something a DJ might use to spin music at a dance club. Each knob and switch allowed for the analog adjustment of some aspect of the display or tactile feedback Dr. Pope would receive from her environment. It was a little old school, but the boxy black board was the type of hardware she'd been building since she first got into video games many years before.

Dr. Pope's intention was to interact with the seemingly sentient locals and to assess their relative intelligence and consciousness based partially on that meeting. She felt that her vast background and experience with A.I. would allow her to more definitively assess whether the creatures inside the simulation were 'thinking' in the human sense, or just cleverly faking intelligence as had been the case with every other so-called A.I. in the past.

Hers was not the only data being used to evaluate the status of these simulated lifeforms. Dr. Davies and Ms. Baxter were building profiles based on the readings they were receiving through the Approximation Engine interface: brain waves, heat signatures, auditory information, and the like. Davies ensured that the readings were being correctly measured, and Baxter crunched that data into something the rest of us could understand.

The physicist, Dr. Walters, was building a comparison document outlining how Aurora's environment differed from Earth's, taking into account variables like gravity — Aurora's was only 92% of Earth's — and how much radiation from their simulated star made it through their simulated atmosphere. Which, it turned out, was significantly less than on Earth.

Miss Deacon leaned against the back wall, alternating

between work on her phone and watching the proceedings with intensity.

I, personally, was enthralled by the process. I'd had the opportunity to be present for numerous NASA projects while working with them in the past, but those events were largely tried-and-true procedures they knew they could safely perform in front of an audience. This was something entirely different. Something which could easily fail, leaving us able to view our simulated universe only from the heavens rather than from the soil. Our data, then, would be greatly limited in scope, and the information with which we proceeded would be forever in question.

To succeed with our infiltration would be incredibly informative. Not only would it allow us to better determine the relative intelligence of this simulated species, it would provide the opportunity to interact with a non-human organism that evolved on another planet, in another solar system, in another universe. It would, in many ways, be our first contact with an alien species.

If the experiment worked. Looking at the cobbled-together VR rig into which Dr. Pope was plugged and entangled, I reminded myself that success was anything but certain.

Michael Hutchins, janitor at Proxy

After we'd first got the virtual reality equipment all set up and pretty well tested, there was a week where the Proxy team would hang around after work hours to play with it. Sometimes they were tryin' stuff out, making sure it worked with the cloud computers they were usin', but sometimes it was more normal stuff. Games my daughter was playin' before she'd went off to school, and which me and the wife would play sometimes, to see how many aliens we could shoot before blowin' ourselves up.

I joined in on a few of the games, but I mostly just watched, like with my daughter. Was fun seein' all them doctors and serious people lettin' loose a little.

I stayed at the office later than usual the night before the big day, helping Dr. Pope put the video game equipment together one more time and making sure all the connections met up right. She told me that if any of the connections were loose, the goggles she put on could be off a little, and just a fraction of a second difference between what the computer was tellin' it to show and what it showed could make her motion sick.

Matthew Gruber, Chief Hardware Specialist at Proxy

We ended up building our own graphics engine to get the resolution right, and added a secondary cell processor to ensure the tech was reading the output from Sunder's simulation correctly. We cobbled together a few dozen high-end cards using a node-network similar to what we did with the Approximation Engine, though it was far simpler and on a way smaller scale.

The end result was sort of a converter between the simulated universe and the OS running on the virtual gear. The universe was the result of physics generated by the Approximation Engine, right? And what we did with the monitors around the office was 'read' that data the same way an eye and brain would: by processing the photons. The trick is that with virtual reality, there's more than just visuals to consider, there's mass. Solid objects. Wind. All kinds of other data that we hadn't been reading as anything more than data. So we needed a way to tell Pope's VR gear that, say, if the data readout showed us a clump of dirt, it should feel like dirt. If the data showed us a strong wind intersecting with her body mass, she'd need to get a different sort of feedback through her gear to tell her that.

We did what we could, but most of the haptics were hacked together pretty quickly. She'd be able to feel the rough outlines of things, and would feel a slight difference between dirt and a strong wind. She'd be able to feel different sensations on different parts of her body. But it would take a lot more time before we could commit the resources to fully fleshing out that interface and doing a decent job of it.

Far more important for our purposes were stability sensations like being able to feel the ground beneath her feet. Very mundane and subtle things like that, which would allow her to act naturally when interacting with the locals.

Dr. Sunder Davies, Simulation Department Head at Proxy

Dr. Pope wanted to see how life-like these artificial lifeforms could be if she interacted with them on their level, a bit like the traditional Turing Test, which was a theoretical means of figuring out if true A.I. had been accomplished.

Nothing against Alan Turing, who was a brilliant mathematician, but the Turing Test concept was utter nonsense. The idea that you could measure intelligence based on a system's cleverness doesn't take complex coding into account. The test had already been beaten numerous times back when we were working on that virtual reality equipment for Dr. Pope, and in each and every case the software in question hadn't actually done anything different from any other software throughout history, it had just been faster and was coded a little better than its predecessors. This resulted in faux A.I.s that were good at approximating the feel and pace of intelligence, but were not actually intelligent.

Dr. Pope knew this. She also knew that her upgraded, one-on-one interactions would only collect a higher caliber of the same type of flawed data. But the data was incredibly relevant to the work we were doing, especially when analyzed in tandem with the other information we were collecting and compiling. If she could be fooled *in situ*, if the digital life we'd evolved in the simulation seemed real to her in a 'real life' situation, then we'd know a lot more about what we were dealing with. We'd know how to treat the maybe-intelligences we'd birthed, and what guidelines we should have in place for future interactions.

We'd also have a better idea of how the A.I.s might play into our business ambitions. Lifelike A.I.s could be used as non-player characters in massively multiplayer online games, for example. Or they could serve as digital concierges on the internet or within consumer electronics. The potential of our artificial life was limitless, and Dr. Pope's VR deep dive would help us decide if and where limits were warranted, and how we might best and most ethically apply them.

Joan Deacon, Chief Financial Officer at Proxy

Amelia wanted to get some face time with the sim-people, and we wanted to make sure that it was time well spent. Which was good, considering the amount of effort and money that was being sunk into the virtual reality setup they were building for her to wear while universe-spelunking. It started out small, but man oh man did her little VR experiment escalate.

To get the most bang for our buck, we decided to wait for the pre-humanoids to turn into full-on, tool-using, art-making humanoids. Human-ish creatures with widespread fire-use and culture, with stone tools. Clothing. The whole nine yards.

Thankfully, our wait-time for that moment was short, in the real-world. The most difficult part was going slow enough so that we cruised through simulated time fast enough for the sims to evolve, but without jumping past all the juicy parts.

So instead of setting a pace of centuries per second as we'd been doing, it was decades. Not long after that, we were going year-by-year.

Stephanie Baxter, Biologist In Residence at Proxy

I worried that my work with Proxy might be done once these virtual humanoids became the dominant life form on Aurora. Most of what was required from that point onward was cultural analysis: anthropology, not biology.

But Dr. Pope set my mind at ease. She told me they'd need me for as long as the company was around. For my observational skills from working in the field and to help evolve other life. If the Aurora project proved fruitful, we'd probably want to do it again. Grow another planet, more species. I could also help guide the company in a new direction, if our current direction didn't work and we needed to return to the drawing board.

Reassured, I returned to my work. I was keeping track of notable events in the timeline of our digital humanoids. Which I was able to do using Dr. Pope's software. It rendered the entire world, and other parts of the solar system, as high-quality graphics. There was some waiting involved if I wanted to render anything outside Aurora's immediate galactic neighborhood, but I could see the entire simulated universe this way, if I wanted. I could zoom out and view the planet in macro, or zoom in and see the pulse on the neck of one of the virtual humanoids from one of the tribes wandering around the planet's main continent.

It was incredible. It was like doing fieldwork, without the risk of accidentally contaminating your site.

Just as on Earth, Aurora's humanoid species reproduced sexually, and with two genders. Their sex organs were significantly different from ours, though, and were tucked up inside their bodies. Folds of skin hid the specifics of their reproductive assets from view, so we imprecisely started calling one of the genders 'male,' because they seemed to have a dominant position within society and greater muscle mass. Unlike human males, however, these Auroran 'males' received their partner's DNA during their reproductive act and carried their young to term. In many ways, the labeling was imprecise. I knew that at some point we'd need to develop more accurate naming conventions for the creatures inhabiting Aurora.

We decided to make Dr. Pope's avatar look like one of their males, and as big and muscle-bound as possible. We wanted to increase the likelihood of her being taken seriously during a pre-civilization period on a world where there was language but no writing. The Aurorans had some simple symbolic iconography they would carve into stone and scribble on walls, but nothing more complex than that.

Dr. Pope would almost certainly have trouble trying to communicate with the locals, and they'd be as confused by her as she was by them. Perhaps even more so. It would be a mutual confusion. How that confusion manifested would tell us a lot. And that's was what she was intending to experience and analyze.

Matthew Gruber, Chief Hardware Specialist at Proxy

Thankfully, Pope had more than a little experience with avatar-building. She wasn't a graphics expert herself, but she was able to mock something up using existing software and some stock renders.

It was tricky, though, building something that would work within the simulation. The life milling around down on Aurora wasn't built using wireframes and pixels and shading engines like you'd find in video games. That was how we were displaying it, but there were actual particles and matter produced by the physics defined by our Approximation Engine, and that meant we'd need an avatar made up of the same to go inside the simulation.

Our universe theoretically allowed for the construction of bio-machines, which were 'empty' humanoid bodies with all the necessary passive biological functions, but no consciousness. We figured we could inhabit one of these biological puppets using signals beamed into the simulation, like cosmic rays, from the real world: our universe would control a biological machine located in their, essentially via remote control.

But because there wasn't anyone inside the simulation, on Aurora, capable of creating such a creature, nor would there be for many generations, we had to build our own empty humanoid in a separate pocket universe. That meant we had to evolve a new species and project it over, atom for atom, which was almost like tearing a hole in one universe to appear in another, but the universes in question were both simulations on the same network of computers, so no wormholes were required.

It wouldn't be pretty, and it would take a hell of a lot of processing power, and it would result in all kinds of uncomfortable matter shifting and reality distortions in Aurora's universe. But we could do it. And we did.

That same week, Amelia hired a full-time psychologist for the team.

Dr. Maxine Richmond, Psychologist In Residence at Proxy

I was hired at Proxy for two main purposes.

The first was to help a staff of high-performers cope with ethical conundrums in their work. Ideally this would be accomplished without killing their productive drive in the tradeoff.

The second was to analyze and assess the mental state of what were being called 'virtual non-entities.' These were simulated minds that could be sufficiently intelligent-seeming that someone with my background would be required to determine whether actual thought was occurring, or just code-based processes and routines of the sort you'd find in most artificial intelligences.

The Proxy team seemed to work well together, and from the outset were welcoming. This is unusual for a small group of people working on a project in secret. Typically, there are more social hurdles to bypass before one can become part of the 'gang.' I surmised that the complex goals they shared lent them this strong connection, and Dr. Pope seemed to instill a confidence in her employees that they were all necessary for success. Their personalities were a volatile combination that could have led to great deal more conflict had Dr. Pope not been in charge.

Dr. Pope was ready to step into the simulation using virtual reality equipment on my first day at the office, and this seemed to be a moment of great trepidation, but also an achievement about which the Proxy employees were quite proud. I would begin my work with the A.I.s, and my efforts would out of necessity be indirect, utilizing the data collected by the staff and by watching the interactions they had with Dr. Pope as soon as contact was established.

Eugene Crisp, Chief Storyteller at Proxy

Dr. Pope's Auroran humanoid body had to be evolved in a smaller, separate universe. This secondary 'pocket' universe was created from a cached version of Aurora's universe, which was then scaled down and manipulated more directly to ensure evolution provided us with what we needed.

What was needed, in this case, was a humanoid species visually similar enough to the Aurorans that they could be mistaken for one another, but with a very specific brain mutation. One that would allow a signal transmitted from the real world through the Approximation Engine's interface to 'occupy' the body. To control its limbs, to sense what it sensed. In other words, a species intentionally evolved to serve as avatars for humans wishing to walk upon Aurora.

Matthew Gruber, Chief Hardware Specialist at Proxy

It took ages to get that damn avatar species evolved correctly. We had to set up millions of micro-universes based on Aurora's, starting from when the Auroran's quadruped ancestors came down from the trees and became bipedal. We culled the simulations that went pretty much exactly the same direction as the main universe, because we didn't want more of the same and we couldn't 'possess' sentient, simulated life. We needed beasties that were more lizard-brain and less pre-frontal cortex. Creatures that evolved to look like the Aurorans, but didn't think so much. We wanted creatures that were all instinct.

We deleted the ones that went wildly astray from the Auroran model, because we needed something that would pass for a local, a body that Pope could wear without being seen as some kind of alien, which might send the Aurorans running for the hills or reaching for weapons.

The lifeforms we eventually evolved looked a lot like the Aurorans. They had the same bipedal stride, shortened thighs and elongated feet that gave them bird-like backwards-knees.

They had tiny little ear canal indentations, spongy olfactory sensors on their chests but no noses, a blue-ish green complexion, and three pairs of opposing digits on each hand, just like the Aurorans.

Importantly, these creatures had a sensitivity to radiation that messed with their motor skills. By assessing what kinds of pulses caused which types of motor-responses, we could pulse radiation into the simulated universe from the real world and take control. Once we figured out what controlled what, the radiation acted like a high-density wireless internet signal which allowed us to control the body through Pope's VR rig. We used the data readouts to determine what matter and waves and such were intersecting which creature, and we converted that info into haptic feedback she could feel.

In retrospect it almost sounds easy, like we just whipped up a custom creature and were ready to go. But it took months of focused work, and there were days when I questioned whether it would turn out as planned. Thankfully, for my sanity and for everyone else's, it did.

Eugene Crisp, Chief Storyteller at Proxy

It was an auspicious morning the day of Dr. Pope's virtual insertion. The sky was clear, squirrels were playing like tiny, fuzzy children around and through the bushes lining the office building, and the entire team was in high spirits. But despite the energetic wind-up, there were complications from the moment Dr. Pope entered the simulation.

She was 'playing' as a very large male of the humanoid

species that dominated Aurora. Dr. Pope controlled his movements with equipment that would look to the untrained eye like deep sea diving gear, or gaming equipment designed by H.P. Lovecraft. The virtual reality apparatus was connected the central simulation interface through what looked like thirty or forty cables.

Dr. Pope planned to 'manifest' about three miles from a camp of locals, a group with which she intended to make contact.

Shoving the mindless puppet hominid from the pocket universe in which he evolved over to the more expansive simulation that housed Aurora required the 'beaming' of particles from the former into the latter. The particles were transmitted as waves into Aurora's simulation and recompiled as particles, which themselves recompiled as our puppet humanoid, on the surface of Aurora.

We knew that the sudden appearance of this matter in an already matter-dense space would result in a sonic boom and perhaps other side-effects, as the local particles shifted to make room for Dr. Pope's avatar. It was decided that three miles should be sufficiently far away from the settlement so that the reverberations wouldn't be noticed by the group of creatures she intended to infiltrate. Unfortunately, while the particle transfer worked, it was imperfectly calibrated. Rather than appearing three miles from the group she wished to visit, she materialized nearly on top of them, just a few feet from their fire, in the center of a circle consisting of over a dozen of their males.

The entire the tribe, including the older children, jumped from their food- and tool-making tasks in response to the thunderclap that accompanied Dr. Pope's appearance. The readings on the simulation interface indicated there was an accompanying smell as well, the unpleasant combination of sulfur and burnt ash. Dr. Pope wouldn't be able to experience that smell firsthand, her sensory equipment being too simple to translate olfactory data, but we knew it was there from data displayed on the non-graphical monitors.

The Auroran humanoids seemed torn between fear and awe. The men clutched at their young, pulling them tighter to their chests and creating a living wall between their young and this unknown threat. The women hefted their weapons, their fingers clenching the carved handles tightly. But not one of them made a move toward this stranger who's sudden appearance was like nothing they'd ever encountered before. They had no experiences to draw upon, no shortcut for understanding, so their fight or flight reflexes hovered somewhere between the two. Our data displayed those competing signals as an increase in specific types of chemical activity throughout their bodies, including parts of their brains.

Dr. Pope hesitated only a moment before deciding to make the most of an imperfect situation. She straightened to her full height, pulled her impressively large shoulders back, and held up one hand toward the tribe, palm forward, six fingers spread. She then turned that hand upward, so that her palm faced the sky. Arm still outstretched, she bowed her head at the tribespeople and waited.

One of their number, a young female, probably in her teens, looked around at her kin, one by one. After a few seconds, she set her weapon, a sharp stone with a carved handle, down on the ground. She then stood back up and repeated the gesture, her palm pointed at Dr. Pope's avatar, fingers spread, then her palm turned skyward. The girl finished by nodding her head.

Dr. Pope smiled. The youth smiled back, her double-rows of sharper-than-human teeth set in a wider-than-human jaw exposed, flashing in a way that would have been menacing out of context, but which in the moment was clearly a reciprocated gesture.

Dr. Pope tapped a finger to her wrist, a gesture that told her software to pull her avatar out of Aurora, converting her matter back into particles and funneling those particles as pure energy back into the cosmos, where they would be pulled from the main simulation back into a pocket universe. The avatar disappeared from the tribal settlement with a thunderclap similar to the one that had announced its arrival.

After the avatar disappeared, the laboratory monitors captured the Auroran girl performing the same wrist-touching gesture that Dr. Pope completed before disappearing.

Dr. Pope pulled off her goggles and stepped away from the virtual reality equipment. She took a deep breath, exhaled, and said, "Well, if they didn't have it before, I think we may have accidentally just given them religion."

Maxine Richmond, Psychologist In Residence at Proxy

It truly was remarkable. This simulated girl responded exactly like a curious youth from the real world might respond. There was no evidence of what Mr. Gruber called 'latency' in the girl's actions. No stutter indicating the necessity to process an unfamiliar experience. No sign of conversion required to compile it to meaningful figures for computation. Just a seemingly instinctual response to a novel situation.

Extraordinary.

Dr. Sunder Davies, Simulation Department Head at Proxy

Dr. Pope's adventure into the simulation was energizing for all of us, but it seemed to have an even greater impact on her.

We began analyzing the responses of the tribe to her presence, individual by individual, and how her god-like arrival and disappearance might influence them over the long-haul.

While we analyzed, Dr. Pope stayed in her office, door shut, a pensive look on her face. She would do that sometimes, when there was a problem to work out. She'd go into hermit-mode. There was a mutual understanding that we'd leave her alone under such circumstances and tend our own gardens. There was plenty to do, and we all had enough responsibility on our own plates to keep us occupied in the meantime.

Joan Deacon, Chief Financial Officer at Proxy

Amelia burst from her office a few days later. Like, actually burst from it, door slamming against the wall and everything. She announced that we'd build a hook. None of us had any idea what she was talking about so she explained.

A 'hook,' she told us, would be an add-on to the software we'd built to manage, document, and display the simulation. This hook software would allow A.I.s within the simulation to 'puncture up,' meaning they'd be able to find this hook, grab hold of it, metaphorically, and be pulled from their simulation within our computers 'up' into the real world. Into our universe.

Matthew Gruber, Chief Hardware Specialist at Proxy

I thought Pope was out of her mind. It was a crazy idea.

I loved it immediately.

How would the hook work?

Amelia wanted to set up a new pocket universe, like the one we used to evolve the puppet humanoid she'd worn while walking around Aurora. An A.I. who managed to 'puncture up,' which was Pope-speak for 'piercing the sky' or something equally romantic-sounding, would be copied, particle for particle, into that pocket universe. They would elevate themselves to another plane of existence.

What would they find in that transcendent pocket universe?

The most direct way to allow the artificial consciousness to actually be in the lab with us would be to rig up some kind of robot body for the A.I. to occupy. The rules in the pocket universe would link the A.I.'s senses to the robot's cameras, ear canals to the robot's microphones, *et cetera*. The result would be an experience much like Pope had when her senses were wired to that of the simulated, burly avatar. Her avatar allowed her to interact with their world, and this avatar would allow them to interact with ours.

Joan in particular was excited about the concept because it brought us a huge step closer to a marketable product. If we could evolve the Aurorans further and help populate their planet with billions of intelligent consciousnesses, we could bring the most capable of those consciousnesses up into the real world to do the kind of work we'd always hoped robots would help us out with. Stuff that required real A.I., not the faked stuff, to do well.

It would be the start of a whole new industry built atop actual A.I., which is what we were increasingly certain we'd created.

Eugene Crisp, Chief Storyteller at Proxy

The team's attention turned to figuring out what shape the hook should take.

It was decided that the hook software should be accessible enough that a simulated consciousness was sure to achieve it within a certain time period, but it also had to be difficult to attain so that the team wouldn't be inundated with up-puncturing A.I.s.

The hook also had to be based on a measurable metric, because it was to be dangled into the simulation until triggered, hence the name. Once accomplished, this achievement would activate the hook, pulling the victorious creature out by copying their consciousness into a pocket universe, much like we'd pulled Pope's avatar back out from the surface of Aurora. From their new home-universe, they would be fed the sensory information their robotic body gathered.

It would be an avatar in reverse, a physical body controlled by a virtual entity.

We watched Aurora evolve from the simulated prehistory in

which Dr. Pope made her appearance until a point that seemed roughly parallel to the European Renaissance on Earth.

In the period between, the Aurorans became almost universally spiritual, organizing around peaceful, internal development-oriented tenets, some of them at first loosely based on the appearance and actions of Dr. Pope's avatar, though the rituals affiliated with that event eventually drifted away into obscurity.

Tribal conflicts escalated into conflicts between villages. Villages became cities, and as these cities were connected by rough-hewn paths and then well-built roads, physical conflict largely ceased, replaced by a spiritual battle of sorts. Cities congregated around core tenets and then chiseled and refined them until they were sufficiently sharp to puncture the beliefs of a rival city. These arguments were delivered by slips of a papyrus-like paper, folded into small, spinning flower-like shapes that were carried to cities with opposing ideologies by men who specialized in making their handmade, message-bearing origami-copters fly further than anyone else.

After at time, one city would convince a sufficient number of citizens in another city of their approach to and interpretations of life, which helped sway the remaining holdouts. In this way, slowly but surely the entire central continent on Aurora came to share the same belief system. The ideas they all shared were centered around a type of meditation similar to some of those practiced on Earth.

The data we received from Aurora indicated that their meditation would sometimes yield practitioners a temporary increase in brain function. Though small, an extra .01% on average, the increased function was even higher for those who meditated regularly. In other words, some of the Aurorans took this element of their faith very seriously and were able to achieve far larger temporary gains to their brain function. Our data showed that .08% had been the greatest-ever gain at the time when we took our measurements.

It was decided this was a reasonable metric to use for the hook. We set the mathematically significant figure of a 1% increase in brain function as the goal to reach. That number was the trigger that, when achieved and recorded by our software, would cause a skilled meditator to be plucked from their simulated-mortal coil and pulled up into our own, into the reality of their creators.

The hook was developed and installed in the simulation software. We sat back and waited for the trigger to snap.

Matthew Gruber, Chief Hardware Specialist at Proxy

We allowed the simulation to play out at about triple real-time-speed from then on. For a long while, nothing happened.

Then, something did.

HOOK

Joan Deacon, Chief Financial Officer at Proxy

We had an alien in our computer.

The guy who caught the hook was different from us, not human. They were relatively small differences, I guess, in terms of culture and biology. Though the lack of a nose was weird, and he breathed through an organ on his chest.

But more importantly he came from another planet, from a solar system that had similar attributes to ours, but was not ours, and…I mean, he was just foreign. Way, way foreign.

Plus? He was living *in a computer*. A virtual person with bird-legs, not a full-on human being. His consciousness and perception of existence and thoughts were all inside a machine. I can't think of anything more alien than that.

Stephanie Baxter, Biologist In Residence at Proxy

Joan had a point, but it didn't seem productive to focus on the differences between our two species rather than the similarities.

Those differences would have to be addressed, though. We could watch these creatures and their culture from above, sure. But we still knew little about them individually. We had no idea how this one in particular would respond to our existence. How he would respond to being plucked from his reality and placed in ours. Or rather, into another reality we controlled.

Matthew Gruber, Chief Hardware Specialist at Proxy

We had the guy who triggered the hook tucked away inside a pocket universe: a sub-universe we evolved separate from the one that contained his world, Aurora.

This universe had land, had air, had all the things a virtual person from Aurora might expect from reality. We were getting pretty good at whipping up smaller universes at that point since we'd done it so many times while iterating the main one. We also had some wonderful cached starting points to work from, so we didn't have to rebuild from scratch each time.

But this little universe had another useful attribute. It was home to a race of 'puppet' humanoids, including the big, burly one Pope had controlled while making first contact with our A.I.s in the main Auroran simulation. That meant we wouldn't have to worry about matter displacement and sonic booms when interacting with hooked Aurorans, because our simulated-biological avatars already lived, quiet and benign as baby deer, exactly where we needed them to be. She could pop in at any time and take control of any one of the thousands of Auroran-like puppet creatures wandering around down there, no inter-universe-travel required.

None of this would have made any sense to the chap we'd pulled up from Aurora and plopped into this other simulation, though. All he knew was that one moment he was meditating in his home, experiencing the only reality he'd ever known, and the next he was sitting in what would look to him like a shrine much like those built by his culture, which were scattered across his continent.

Even if his eyes had been open when he transitioned, which they weren't, it would have been a seamless move from his perspective. We copied his whole consciousness from one universe to the other, and the copy only 'activated' when it was fully compiled in the new location. So from his point of view, he picked up right from where he left off with no latency in between, despite the five or so seconds it took in real life, in the lab, to make the switch. One moment at home, and the next moment, whoosh! Gone. He exists inside some kind of temple. In a temple and about to meet his maker.

Maxine Richmond, Psychologist In Residence at Proxy

There were several considerations guiding our planning of the initial encounter between Dr. Pope and this young man from Aurora. The first was that he would need to feel safe and experience a sense a familiarity with his environment. Hence, the shrine.

Another was that he would need to feel that the transition between his reality and the new reality in which he found himself was seamless. I believe the technology used addressed this concern.

Some changes were made to the original plan because of the third consideration, that there would need to be a sense of continuity between this young man's consciousness in his reality, and that which he experienced in the pocket universe into he was pulled.

Eugene Crisp, Chief Storyteller at Proxy

By achieving a 1% increase in brain function through meditation, the A.I. had activated the hook software, which then copied him into the smaller, so-called pocket universe the Proxy team had created.

But the copying process did not 'remove' him from Aurora. The young man existed in both his own world and in the pocket universe simultaneously. Time within his home universe was slowed to an almost imperceptible speed from the perspective of those of us in the lab, which was mirrored in the pocket universe that he was pulled into. So he wasn't missing much time by being pulled away. A fraction of a second.

But the copying was still a problem. If we were to send him back to Aurora after the meeting, his brain changed by the experience, changed by the new information and environmental variables he encountered while there, we would have to 'kill' the existing version of him back home in order to 'update' his existence in a seamless fashion. Otherwise, the Aurora version of him would grow in one direction, and the hooked version would grow in another, and we would find ourselves with two separate entities rather than one who has experienced two different universes.

Maxine Richmond, Psychologist In Residence at Proxy

The question of making copies of a person raised several moral questions that I felt would distract the team in an unproductive manner.

For example, if we could copy these people from the simulation, people who were evolved in the same way we were and based on the same physics and compounds and biology, could we , then, be copied? Could multiple instances of our consciousnesses exist at the same time and be replicated in, say, a nearby computer? Or a robot? And what would that mean for our sense of self? For the ability to say, "I am me?" Would that ability be erased? Expanded upon?

I raised this point with Dr. Pope in private, and she agreed that it wasn't something we should fixate on just yet. She decided, and I agreed, that the most ideal stopgap solution was to build a 'sleep switch' into the hook system, which would put the A.I. who triggered the software into a coma-like trance for the duration of their up-puncturing, shutting down their brain until their consciousness was returned to it.

It was an imperfect solution, but the best of bad options.

Matthew Gruber, Chief Hardware Specialist at Proxy

The sleep switch was kind of like the DRM, the digital rights management software, that's sometimes installed in digital music or ebooks to keep those files from being used by more than one device at a time.

It's technically possible to copy digital information, including simulated consciousnesses, an infinite number of times, but because of the software changes we made there could only ever be one version of a consciousness in existence across all universes at a time within simulations using our Approximation Engine.

Dr. Sunder Davies, Simulation Department Head at Proxy

To me, the most interesting thing about the sleep switch was that it allowed us to play with temporality even more than we already could. We already had a great deal of control over time as it existed within the simulation. We could fly through centuries or eons in the blink of an eye, and we could revert to a cached time period 3,000,000 years in the past just as quickly. We couldn't easily rewind time to step backward; our only option there was to revert to an earlier, cached simulation state. But beyond that we weren't limited in our control of in-simulation time.

What the sleep switch allowed us to do was 'abduct' someone from their reality and pull them into ours, and to keep them with us for as long as we liked without it impacting their lives back home. We could copy a sleeping A.I. into our pocket universe and keep them with us for days or weeks or a lifetime, only to return them to their sleeping selves back home before the next morning, their memories full of what they'd experienced, but their bodies the same as they left them. In the case of our hook-triggering meditator, this meant we could return them to their body before the end of a meditation session.

The sleep switch gave us the power to make contact while disrupting their lives as little as possible. It also gave us the option to leave them wondering if it was all just a dream, should we need to. The mind boggled at the possibilities.

Eugene Crisp, Chief Storyteller at Proxy

One of many tricky practical issues we faced before the first A.I. punctured up was how to communicate with them beyond simple gestures.

Body language, facial expressions, and pointing were all useful bits of shared language, and they were how Pope was able to interact with the early Aurorans she'd met. But more complex symbolism would be necessary if we wanted to establish a relationship with this entity, and figure out how it fit into what we were trying to accomplish as a business and whether these intelligences would be capable of working with the people of Earth as virtual assistants, characters in video games, or even just as ambassadors from one culture to another.

Matthew Gruber, Chief Hardware Specialist at Proxy

Pope and I began customizing translation software that would learn as we learned, and which we hoped would help bridge the language gap. It would start as a kind of interactive game, where the A.I. and Pope, through her avatar, would point at objects and exchange the words they used to describe these things. This was off-the-shelf software we'd customized, by the way, just white-label stuff we were able to get a good deal on through one of our investors, who'd put money in the company that made it.

Our software would create a dictionary of terms and help us learn the sentence structure, moving into verbs, concepts, and more as time went by. If the abductee kept up with the game, he would learn our language, as well. He could then share that knowledge with his fellow Aurorans by teaching classes or publishing some kind of guide inside the simulation.

The locals had a written language we didn't yet understand, and their version of books, which differed from ours primarily in how they were bound — they used a woven mesh to hold pages together at the spine — were the best possible media available in their time period for sharing and distributing the information we wanted them to know *en masse*.

Having a local publish such a book would eliminate the issues involved with projecting stuff into their universe from another universe. The sonic booms wouldn't be a problem, then, nor would the potential long-term quantum disruption of their planet, which was something we began to worry about after we noticed some errant figures in our physics numbers, post-prehistorical-Pope-visit. It looked like every time we broke the rules of their reality, there was a chance that something could terribly wrong with their physics, and that was something we wanted to avoid. So we couldn't inject objects into their world anymore.

But knowledge? Knowledge we could do. If we could teach them, and learn more about how they communicated and operated, they'd become our information mules, hauling stashes of awesome across the borders of our universes.

Dr. Sunder Davies, Simulation Department Head at Proxy

The environment in which Dr. Pope met the A.I. was simple, but practical. It felt the same as the 'real world' to the simulated young man, and was displayed for the rest of us on lab monitors in the same photo-realistic way his universe was.

Dr. Pope experienced it in the same way she'd perceived Aurora, through her VR equipment.

There was something surreal about the place, though it wasn't instilled with that surreality intentionally. Here was a place built solely to house a conversation between two intelligent species. A place intended to sand down the rough edge inherent in a meeting between beings from different realities. A place that would serve as background during a meeting between creator and creation.

Layers upon layers of complexity.

We did our best to preemptively address any difficulties that might arise, and those efforts did not go unrewarded. Or, it turned out, unrecognized by the young Auroran who opened his eyes to find himself there.

Maxine Richmond, Psychologist In Residence at Proxy

The young man seemed to comprehend more than he was showing, outwardly. We could 'see,' through the data on our monitors, that there was plenty going on inside his brain of which he wasn't giving any physical indication.

We could see his adrenaline spikes and the activity levels in different sections of his species' version of a prefrontal cortex. We could gauge his level of alarm at finding himself in an unfamiliar setting and in the presence of Dr. Pope's avatar, who was a very large, muscular specimen. He was panicked like someone who was aware of danger, but also aware that panicking wouldn't contribute anything positive to the situation.

His body was still, his breathing regular, but his mind was racing, leaping, trying to make sense of this novel scenario, like a butterfly bumping against the fringes of a room to assess its dimensions. He was trying to bring order to the disorder of the world around him, and he was doing so without even a twitch of his hairless lip or a flutter of his long-lashed eyelid.

Eugene Crisp, Chief Storyteller at Proxy

Dr. Pope sat in the same manner as the young man, his legs folded beneath him like the hind legs of a dog. This relaxed kneel was common among his people, suitable for extended meditation sessions. She waited silently while he adjusted to his circumstances.

They sat inside a small building about the size of a two-bedroom apartment, but one with an entirely open floorplan.

The architecture was all structural curves and jointed beams, the colors calming beiges and off-whites. Natural light filtered in through a semi-transparent sheet of papyrus-like paper, casting a warm glow throughout the space that was reflected from the curves of the walls and ceilings, abolishing all but the slightest hint of shadows.

There was a small case, reminiscent of an under-counter wine rack and carved from a wood-like substance the Aurorans harvest from their native shrubs, weaving it together and then compressing it into a carvable density. This case contained fifty tiny shelves, and upon each shelf was a folded piece of their papyrus, origami'd into flying flower shapes to indicate that the material contained writings of spiritual significance.

It was fortuitous that proficiency in meditation was chosen as the key metric for the hook, because the young man proved quite flexible in adjusting his mental state to his circumstance. He seemed to accept the new, unlikely reality in which he found himself, and acted in accordance with that accepted truth.

Once it was clear the young man wouldn't jump out of his skin with fear, Dr. Pope held out her hand, palm toward him, then lifted the palm upward. It was the gesture of greeting she'd used the first time she'd gone down into the simulation, and it was a gesture that had, over the course of many simulated generations, become a *de facto* symbol of goodwill among Aurorans, akin to a handshake or smile.

The young man repeated the gesture in kind. Dr. Pope then pointed at herself and said, "Pope."

The young man breathed deeply, paused, then pointed at himself and said, "Grenn." To confirm, Dr. Pope pointed at the young man and said, "Grenn." He pointed at her and said, "Pope."

From the moment in which they'd established the game they were playing, communication was a matter of going from item to item in the room and identifying it in their respective vocabulary.

Though there was little in the way of furniture in the spartan space, there was an organized clutter of objects that were determined to be important for a foundational understand of the Auroran tongue. The objects were also chosen based on cultural parallelisms between universes. Aurora didn't have a fruit that was visually similar to an apple, for example, but they did have a family of plants that were quite similar to shrubs. They didn't have much in the way of insects, but they did have a vast assortment of cat-like mammals. As such, there was a simulated cat species present, white with black spots, peeking at the kneeling ambassadors from behind a potted hedge.

After two hours of back and forth naming of things, the dictionary-building software keeping track of the many translations, Dr. Pope nodded and again performed greeting she had opened with, palm forward then upward.

Grenn did the same, but slowly. He seemed hesitant to finish, and after he did, he spoke slowly in his own tongue. His exact words were not yet translatable, but his facial expression spoke volumes. His eyes were darting around the room, across Dr. Pope's face, trying to take it all in before it disappeared.

He didn't want this strange dream to end. He wondered if this would be the last time he'd encounter this mysterious teacher who was also a student. Wondered if this would be the last glance he'd have of this strange place and the strange spotted cat he'd scratched behind the ears.

Dr. Pope noticed this. She pointed at Grenn, then put her

hands together and laid her head on them, closing her eyes as if she were sleeping. She then pointed at where she was seated. The implication was: go to sleep to come here.

Grenn nodded. He closed his eyes and made the same sleeping gesture, then spread his arms to encompass the whole of the shrine they occupied before pointing at the mat upon which he was seated. I sleep, I end up here.

It seemed like as good a time as any to end the meeting. Dr. Pope tapped her wrist, a gesture that meant 'farewell' on Aurora, and Grenn tapped his own.

He was pulled from the micro-universe and returned to his body in the main simulation. He occupied the same body as before, but his brain had changed, and the version that had traveled to the pocket universe overwrote the version that had been left there, comatose. The new memories were incorporated into his grey matter, and his brain was subtly but instantly reshaped.

At the lab, the team gathered around a monitor that showed Grenn's comatose, but seemingly meditating body, to see what he would do when he awoke.

Grenn opened his eyes and looked around his empty room, the room where he'd kneeled down to meditate twenty minutes previous, Aurora-time. He took a deep breath, looked at his hands, and looked up at the ceiling, toward the sky.

He smiled as he squinted up at the diffuse light filtering through his papyrus skylight, up toward the sky through which he had punctured.

Stephanie Baxter, Biologist In Residence at Proxy

We pulled Grenn up into the pocket universe again, not long after that initial meeting.

It was only the next night for him, but it had been a full month for us. Having control over the universe you're interacting with offers distinct advantages. It allows you to seem far more prepared and put together than you actually are, for example.

We had mountains of data to wade through. Tidal waves of raw numbers to crunch and compile and make sense of, and just as many qualifiable readings to take. All in an attempt to work up an emotional and psychological outline for Grenn, which we hoped to use as a baseline for his humanoid race as a whole.

What we learned was remarkable and heartening. It appeared that despite the physical differences between Aurorans and humans, most of the fundamental aspects of how our bodies and genetics work were the same.

We were hoping this would be the case. We rigged his planet so that life there would work from the same basic blueprints as life on Earth, so that an intelligent species evolving there would be as close to *homo sapien* as possible. So that the A.I.s would be useful to us in the real world.

Before we had the new data, I think several people on the Proxy team believed there would be a greater gulf between us and the Aurorans than there was. There were variations in organ type and size, and physical differences in where our sensory equipment was located and how our joints fit together. There were also circulatory system dissimilarities: the Aurorans had a more efficient neurological 'cleansing system,' for example which allowed them to live a few years longer than humans, and thrive on less sleep

But it was all based on the same underlying principles. Grenn's species didn't eat magma or breathe chlorine. They were different shapes but made out of similar parts. Different arrangements, but still products of carbon-based, mammalian Legos.

Maxine Richmond, Psychologist In Residence at Proxy

There were, of course, a large number of cultural differences between Earth-born humans of the modern age and a young man pulled from a spiritualism-based culture experiencing the technological equivalent of our European Renaissance on a planet that has never seen extreme examples of war.

Grenn seemed a very capable person in that he adjusted his thinking patterns to suit his situation. He was able to calm himself quickly and reliably, and when faced with the unfamiliar, which was an inescapable reality of his interactions with Dr. Pope's avatar no matter how comfortable we tried to make him, he embraced the novelty and learned from it rather than recoiling and retreating toward mental conservatism.

Matthew Gruber, Chief Hardware Specialist at Proxy

The next step was to educate this kid to a sufficient degree that we could safely bring him into our universe. The real world.

I'd just finished up the final touches on a different type of pocket universe, one that would plug the inhabitants' senses into hardware. The data we were collecting about Grenn was of vital immediate importance because I needed to figure out how to connect his visual senses to a camera, and how to attach the part of his brain that perceived sound up to a microphone.

We wanted to build a robot that an A.I. from one of these simulations could occupy, a move that would open all kinds of doors in making these consciousnesses practical in the real world. It would also be a major psychological victory to bring an intelligence from a universe we'd built 'up' to our level. Into our lab. How utterly cool would that be?

So while Amelia taught the kid English, and Stephanie documented all of Grenn's minuscule physical differences, and Maxine mapped out his psychological state, Sunder was helping me translate their work into this pocket universe-plus-robot synthesis. Jim helped out quite a bit, too, because it turned out that you need to have a solid understanding of physics to build a universe without traditional physics.

Pope could occupy a digital avatar of a humanoid that looked like Grenn's species, so it seemed only fair that Grenn should have the chance to occupy a robotic avatar that looked like us. The science fiction aspirations of humanity, worn like a suit by a creature from a simulated planet.

WITHIN

Dr. Sunder Davies, Simulation Department Head at Proxy

Grenn had lived his life on a planet, in a culture, and during a technological time period in which many empirically incorrect things were 'true' based on the level of knowledge his people had accumulated.

For instance, prevailing wisdom by Auroran experts held that disease was caused by imbalances in one's 'essence,' which was a word they used to describe everything from psychological instability to discontentment with the taste of one's food. Much like the information gathered by humans in the time period to the European Renaissance, his people were remarkably close to the truth in some aspects of their understanding, but way, way off in others.

From that baseline of comprehension, Grenn would be entering our world. A world of technology. A world that would likely seem to be set far in the future from his standpoint.

Eugene Crisp, Chief Storyteller at Proxy

Grenn's was a society fixated on the pursuit of intellectual and spiritual enlightenment. The human version of enlightenment, in contrast, has more often focused on improving our mastery of the arts, science, and technology.

Dr. Pope often reminded us that Grenn was, for all intents and purposes, a young man from the past. This was shorthand, of course, and didn't account for many important details. But as a heuristic it worked. Dr. Pope was trying to reassure us that we'd have more in common with Grenn's people than might seem likely, and thinking about his transition in those terms, a scenario presented and revisited numerous times in books and film, allowed us to predict what aspects of our world might seem unintelligible to our visitor and how best to make those elements more transparent.

Maxine Richmond, Psychologist In Residence at Proxy

Grenn was learning English at an impressive clip. We couldn't be certain if his polyglot propensity was a gift he had as an individual, or if his culture's predilection for internal dialogue and self-exploration, and his brain's disproportionately prefrontal cortex-centered arrangement, had wired his brain to more quickly absorb symbol-based information. Either way, he was well-prepared for his visit to Earth in terms of language, which allowed us to focus on preparing him in other ways.

We had considered bringing Grenn to our universe as soon as he could speak our language passingly, with no further pocket universe-based preparation. This would allow for his education to take place in context.

I argued against this emphatically. Despite the young man's calm in the face of novel and disconcerting situations leading up to that point, he had still occupied his own body throughout his lessons, and existed in a world that seemed like his own. He had also been taught by someone who appeared to be his species.

He was going to occupy a robotic body and interact with strange creatures from another world, while in another world. His resolve would be challenged with far more intensity than it had been previously.

Grenn would also struggle with cultural and technological discord. Being exposed to everyday things we take for granted, such as electricity, could shake his calm and send him into a psychosis. Far better, I argued, to present him with an introduction to Earth first, along with its accompanying realities, and to slowly introduce these concepts one by one, just as we'd done with language.

Joan Deacon, Chief Financial Officer at Proxy

I'd been oh-so-subtly nudging the team toward HPR activities, which were actions and investments that had a 'high potential reward.'

When Amelia decided to use a significant chunk of our seed capital to buy a robot company, I was skeptical. That's maybe a nice way of saying it. I sort of thought it might be one of Matthew's pie-in-the-sky, science fiction fantasy moves, which would allow him to play with robots and have fun while the company's money slowly slipped away. That kind of spending happened within a lot of high-tech businesses when they focused on making 'cool,' but not HPR, acquisitions and investments.

I learned a bit more about what Amelia had planned, though, and it started to make sense. In fact, it didn't just make sense: it struck me that this, *this* was the direction we should be moving. Robots controlled by simulation-grown intelligences. It was so obvious that I'd somehow overlooked it.

I couldn't stop thinking up new business models that would make use of this unique value proposition we'd be building for ourselves. Virtual and real world crossover video games, where you could compete in a simulated world like a video game, but also in real life with opposing teams controlling drones or A.I. laser tag bots or whatever.

Or robo-pets that were actual animals, evolved and born in another universe. Entire planets of critters, beamed into the real world. The bodies they inhabited would be custom, well-padded and fuzzy robotic animal bodies. The animal intelligences themselves would be evolved to be adorable and lovey-dovey. They'd be the perfect companions, and they wouldn't eat you out of house and home or poop all over the place. You could even upgrade and update your pet! Put it in a different body when you get sick of the one you've got.

Even better, you could drop into their universe, onto their world, and virtually catch your own pet before bringing them back up to the real world and into your home. It'd be like a high-concept Pokémon game, with robots and higher price tags. Pig-lizards for everyone!

Or how about crossover rooms, where the real world and virtual world overlapped, and you could exist in both simultaneously? This could be particularly useful for restaurants, high-end hotels, spas, and, um, businesses that cater to, ah, adult audiences. Places where you want real, live people to be able to interact with simulated A.I.s in two worlds at the same time, with an intuitive means of splicing those two worlds together.

So when Amelia told me that the process of bringing Grenn over would be slow, that we'd be taking our time and working on the robotic tech required to make him comfortable on Earth, I was all about it. I tried to play it cool, as if I was giving in, giving them what they wanted just because I'm nice. But I think they could tell I was excited.

Eugene Crisp, Chief Storyteller at Proxy

Grenn's acclimation process began with the installation of a monitor in the same pocket universe-based temple where Dr. Pope's avatar met with Grenn for their language exchange sessions.

There was some discussion about bringing simulated replications of each item we wanted to discuss into the little shrine, but decided it would be less intimidating if the objects were kept at a perceptual arm's length. There were also some concepts that wouldn't be easy to explain using props. Though we weren't as concerned about the long-term physical integrity of our pocket universe as the one containing Aurora, we were keen to avoid overt destruction to the home-world of our puppet Auroran-like species for as long as possible. As such, the projection of just one object, the monitor and its accompanying electronics package, was a simpler, safer, and far more elegant option than the alternative.

Sitting across one from another in the shrine, Grenn maintained his usual calm when Dr. Pope turned on the monitor, and didn't blink as she used it to display images from his world. He seemed to understand that he was seeing a representational image, not a tiny box filled with a tiny world, which was a good start.

Next, there was an 'evolution of technology' presentation, which was essentially just a fancy slideshow with animations and videos that Mr. Gruber and Dr. Davies put together over the course of a week. Grenn watched as simple tools made way for machinery, and it was explained how machinery had, on Earth, led to social change. We emphasized the point with examples from his world, which meant focusing on agricultural tools, as farming was a trade most of his people were at least minimally familiar with, and the tools were common enough on Aurora for him to recognize them despite not personally having had any farming experience.

Then came a difficult leap. We wanted to explain how the mechanical technologies he had been shown could lead to things like electronics, microprocessors, and virtual reality. But there were no parallels to these things in his world, so we had to explain these concepts almost completely within the context of technology from our world.

This took the discussion beyond the realm of slideshows. Dr. Pope spent days with Grenn, covering everything from punch cards to hydrogen bombs. Throughout, she avoided any mention of the fact that Grenn and his universe were simulations existing within machines that we'd built. Instead, she told him that there were many universes, and that things worked a bit differently in each of them. He came from one universe, and she came from another. The way people are and the tools they use, she explained, differ based on what kinds of plants and animals they have, what kind of weather is prevalent where those technologies were developed, and so on.

Grenn was clearly enthralled by the idea of a 'planet,' and she spent some time clarifying that, yes, his planet was round, and yes, that meant if you sailed in one direction long enough you'd eventually end up back where you started. Yes, her planet worked the same way. No, they didn't know of any planets that deviated from that model.

Planets and punchcards were fairly straightforward. Other concepts were trickier, in part because there was little to build upon other than the images and videos presented on the screen.

Explaining the screen itself, for example, was a difficult feat. When Dr. Pope first informed him that the rectangular thing would show him real objects that actually existed, he wanted to know by what mechanism it was able to do this. Dr. Pope asked him how he thought it might work, after showing him a still image of a tractor. He studied the image for a moment, then proposed that it might have something to do with focusing one's mental energy through some kind of crystal. Dr. Pope's thoughts were perhaps being projected onto the large, polished facet of this special crystal.

His answer made clear what we were dealing with. His was a world very much like our own, but to his civilization, technology had always played second chair to spirituality, meditation, and other inward-facing pursuits. The study of crystals and 'spiritual technology' was a popular field of study among the intelligentsia of Aurora. We humans were more likely to change our environments than change ourselves, but Grenn's was a species that looked inward almost constantly, and outward only on rare occasions.

Matthew Gruber, Chief Hardware Specialist at Proxy

The kid made some good headway into the fundamentals those first few weeks. It's not that I didn't believe he could do it, it's more that I didn't think he would take so kindly to all these concepts we were throwing at him.

Coming from a world of meditators and monks, okay, sure, I guessed he probably wouldn't lash out with physical violence when faced with the unfamiliar. I supposed that whatever he learned from Pope he would accept as one of many possible truths. But having zero background in technology, I didn't think he'd be able to make the connections he made. And I really didn't think he'd show such enthusiasm for tech. After a few educational get togethers, for which we stole him from his sleep, night after Auroran night, he was asking the kinds of questions I would expect from a first year engineering student.

Given that Grenn came from a world without metallurgy or electricity or any of the other key components of modern engineering, it was damn impressive.

Maxine Richmond, Psychologist In Residence at Proxy

After many weeks of very hard work, which took place nightly for Grenn, though only weekly for the staff so that we might prepare between meetings, we'd reached a point where the young man was ready to be brought into the real world. To have the virtual veil pulled from his eyes, if we're being poetic, so that he might see things as they truly are.

Dr. Pope explained this to him. Explained that she was going to bring him to her world, which was a completely different world from his. A world that was similar, but had existed much longer, and as a result contained the technologies and concepts she'd been showing him. She explained that the body he knew as her was just an illusion created by clever technology, and that he would encounter her as she actually was, in her own body. He'd also meet her team, a group of people who knew a great many things about the technologies they'd been discussing. She asked him if he was ready.

Without hesitation, he nodded. "Yes," he said, in accented English, a slight lisp tugging on his consonants. "I look forward to seeing your world, Pope."

That was that. He was ready, we were ready, and a simple, high-end robot body was ready.

Eugene Crisp, Chief Storyteller at Proxy

A young man, approximately twenty-five Auroran years old, fell into a coma while sleeping one night. His body was scanned, and all of his particles, including the chemicals and electrical impulses triggering in his brain at the moment he went comatose, were copied to a pocket universe simulated by the same machine that catalyzed and housed his world, but partitioned off as a separate segment and given very different rules.

Most traditional physics did not apply inside this smaller simulation, and if you were to perceive what your eyes saw, your ears heard, your tongue tasted, and your nerves felt, you would go mad due to the lack of sensory information. Mass did not exist in this pocket universe, or at least not in the same way it existed on Aurora.

Instead, there was a simulacrum. A body of metal and polymer and a few bits of heat-resistant ceramic which connected to the pocket universe wirelessly. It was physically located in the Proxy machine shop, one room over from the laboratory where the young man's interactions had been tracked and studied since he first triggered the hook software that was dropped into his reality by his creators.

A digital individual brought to this massless pocket universe would be, by default, 'plugged in' to the robot's sensory and acoustic equipment. Sound vibrations would be received through a microphone located on the robot's head and converted into nerve impulses in the brain, cameras would transduce photons into neural impulses, delivering them to the brain just as retinas would, and the Broca's area of the simulated brain — or rather, the Auroran equivalent of the same — would conduct grammatical processing and trigger a speech program which allowed the robot to speak.

Matthew Gruber, Chief Hardware Specialist at Proxy

How would the kid respond to occupying the robot body?

We had no idea. His 'consciousness' would be projected into the bot, his actual simulated particles and whatnot would be stored in a separate universe. To him, it would seem like the robot arm was his arm, the robot cameras were his eyes, and that would mean he'd feel numb in a lot of ways. Instead of having a barrage of information flooding his senses, like the air on his skin and the myriad range of tactile sensations on his fingertips, he'd 'see' a certain resolution of vision, 'hear' a specific decibel-range, and 'feel' a very limited number of pressure sensations in his hands. These finger inputs would tell his brain that he was touching something, but only when encountering sufficient resistance in the fingers, and only with a spectrum of a few dozen pressure levels.

The technology was fairly advanced for a robot at that time. Not the absolute top of the line, but, well, we weren't certain it was necessary to buy the barn at that point. It was sufficiently sophisticated machinery to try our reverse-avatar concept out, but we knew Grenn would feel like he was encapsulated, confined, and muffled in many ways. Pope tried to prepare him for the experience, and she did a good job. When we got him inside the pocket universe and hooked him up to the bot, he seemed more curious than panicked.

It only took a few seconds, but frankly it was a big victory that he was in there at all, so there were smiles all around when it worked. We weren't certain how well the transfer would go, because although we knew we could house him in the smaller simulated universe with the shrine, projection of sensory information from hardware to a simulation was, as of then, mostly untested. It was a really great theory with a few experimental case-studies on the books, but a lot of things work in theory and in the lab, but not so much in real life.

But this worked, and all we had to do once he was in there

was adjust the inputs and outputs so that he wasn't deaf or deafened, and wasn't whispering or shouting every word. Volume up, volume down. That kind of thing. We also limited his range of movement until we could be sure that he wouldn't go all Terminator on us.

Joan Deacon, Chief Financial Officer at Proxy

I don't think there was any real danger of someone being hurt. No one real, I mean. From the real world. There was a chance, from what Matthew told me, that Grenn could be lost somewhere along the way, lost in digital transit. But there was a chance of that from the beginning, even when we brought him out of the simulated world into the tiny one with the shrine where Amelia met with him and taught him English.

The real problem would have been if Grenn was transferred to this new universe they'd grown, only to find his senses didn't exist because they didn't plug into the robot correctly.

He could only sense things through the connection established with the robot, right? So it would have been a major problem if the connection didn't work, or didn't work as intended. He would've been a brain stuck in this universe of nothingness, and that's the type of thing that could drive a person insane. Not just because he'd exist in nothingness, but because according to Matthew, time wouldn't even exist there because he was meant to experience time through his senses, which in his case meant through the robot, in the real world.

So if the connection hadn't worked, Grenn's mind would have been stuck in nothingness for what would have seemed to him like forever. An infinite amount of time in a void. Kind of messed up, and I'm glad it didn't happen, because I'm pretty sure that's how robotic serial killers are made.

Stephanie Baxter, Biologist In Residence at Proxy

There's never been a biological entity that experiences life through another body not directly connected to their brain. There are some parasites that are able to detect the reactionary chemicals that their hosts release in response to external stimuli, but that's just a shadow of a hint of what we had with Grenn and the robot.

When the robot moved its head, for the first time ever life from a virtual world was existing in the real world. This entity, who was a young man, regardless of where he grew up, was a pioneer. He had 'punctured up,' to use the terminology coined by Matthew and Dr. Pope. He existed on a universal plane higher than his own.

The question of what this all meant on a larger scale, if anything, came up almost immediately.

Michael Hutchins, janitor at Proxy

Mr. Gruber asked me to stay late for their big day, which for me meant stayin' early, since I typically worked a night shift and would be sticking 'round till late mornin' to help them set up the robot they were tryin' out for the first time.

It was the first time connected to their artificial intelligences,

I mean. Not the absolute first time. Mr. Gruber just loved takin' things apart and putting them back together again, and he'd sometimes make 'em even better than they started, when he did. He stuck around late a few times. He always said he lost track of time, but I could tell he was waitin' for me to show up because the work he was doin' required another steady hand, and someone with a knack for the way machines go together.

So we'd played around with the robot a few times, fillin' it up with different programs from different companies, some that made their own robots, and some that were meant to go on phones or computers. One of them was made for cars, and kept complainin' because we wouldn't buckle our seat belts, though we had no seat belts to buckle, and no way to tell it so.

This new program they were puttin' in the robot was something they'd been working on for a while. I knew a little bit about it because I'd seen some drawings and charts they'd left on their whiteboards and desks overnight, and it looked like they'd build some big, big world inside the 'cloud computer' they invented. Some kind of fancy new type of program that was meant for robots, looked like.

But Mr. Gruber, he told me that they'd made a whole world inside that computer, a whole universe, and that they had a person from that computer world ready to join us while wearing the robot. That this person was a program, but one that was more like us than like those phone and car assistants everyone was using.

Well I was very interested in seein' that, and I told him so. And he said he was happy that was the case, because he was hopin' I'd help him triple-check the connections so that nothin' went sideways during the test.

Dr. Sunder Davies, Simulation Department Head at Proxy

After Michael helped Matthew check the sensory equipment on the 'robatar,' which was the truly lame name Matthew was calling the robot avatar, Dr. Pope confirmed everything was ready. She activated the software that pulled Grenn up from his world and into ours.

Our heads swiveled in unison, from the monitor showing Grenn asleep on his floor mat in his home on Aurora, to the robatar that had been resting quietly on the other side of the room, the only occupant of a cleared out space, nothing but air in robo-arm range.

The robatar's head tilted up and the activation lights in its eyes flicked on. The head rotated left to right, then right to left. It pivoted its head on its neck, like a yogi preparing to stretch, seemingly unaware of anything beyond these simple movements it was making. Its arms twitched, then lifted just an inch, then moved quickly, arms bent at the elbow, flapping like a bird. Matthew and Joan both stifled laughs, but there were smiles on all the faces in the room. Except the robatar's, which was incapable of that type of expression, its featureless face able to display digital features, but those disabled for the purposes of this initial introduction. It would take a lot more work before we could figure out how to sync that feature up with Grenn's brain-signals that would trigger facial movements.

Finally, the robatar's movements slowed, then stopped, and the face pointed at us, the brightly lit eyes pointed at the center of our group. I remembered that the eye-lenses were wide-angle, so he could probably see all of us without needing to turn his head.

We went through a round of introductions, and we stuck with verbal introductions, no handshakes, to keep things simple, and because the robatar's movements were limited. He nodded to each of us after we spoke our names and nodded at him. We looked quite different from him and his species, but then, we also lived in another universe. He seemed to take these differences as he took all of the other shocks he'd been exposed to since we made first contact: calmly and with quiet reserve.

Dr. Pope introduced herself last, and it was the only introduction that seemed to take Grenn aback. She seemed to be expecting his pause. She explained that going disguised as her avatar had been a necessity because she had first visited his world many, many generations previous. Back then, to be taken seriously and not attacked by the locals, she had to be an impressive enough specimen by their standards that she held their attention and inspired awe.

She asked him if he understood, and he said that he did, somewhat, but could not understand how a person could be another person, and how it was that she could live long enough to have visited both his ancient ancestors and him.

This was the meat of the conversation we'd wanted to have, which all the earlier explanations about technology had been leading up to. Grenn listened quietly, nodding his metal head from time to time in understanding, and sometimes tilting it slightly to the side in a robotic, but still remarkably human look of befuddlement.

When Dr. Pope had finished explaining that his world was a simulation built in our world using technology, and that therefore he was a product of selective evolution, and perhaps not 'real' in the same sense as we were, but still very 'real' in the sense that he was an evolved, physics-based, living thing, Grenn asked a question none of us were expecting.

Matthew Gruber, Chief Hardware Specialist at Proxy

"How could you do it?" Grenn asked. "If we are life, as you have said, no different from your life except in how our…matter… was created, how could you justify intentionally destroying our entire universe so many times?"

Honestly? It was a damn good question. And not one I'd ever thought to ask.

Building something like this from scratch, where the first steps are just concepts and theories, and the later stages are the only parts that actually result in tangibles, you don't always connect the dots as well as you should. The dots we were missing, clearly, were some pretty heavy philosophical ones.

For example, if we created something that was alive, how much responsibility did we have for that life? If we, say, deleted a universe and restarted it from a cache — which was just a saved, frozen instance of that universe from a different point in their history — did we commit genocide by doing so? Did we obliterate their entire species, and their reality, only to start up a different version of that universe that we might also destroy later?

In a way, and I'm not proud of this, but in a way I was happy to be just the hardware guy at that moment. Because that meant that maybe I was less responsible for answering those questions. I like a challenge, and I like making waves and pushing boundaries, but I sure as hell didn't have a good answer for Grenn.

Stephanie Baxter, Biologist In Residence at Proxy

We were gobsmacked when Grenn asked us about the selective evolution of his universe. I don't think any of us had thought about it from that perspective before.

Which made sense. To us it was just...not a game, but similar to one. Simulated reality has always been far from actual reality. I think we were all approaching this technology as just another variation on that theme. A better pretend world, but still a pretend world.

Even in my own case this was true, and I closely studied the life in the simulated universe, Grenn and his people included. I helped cull and breed their ancestors. Helped to guide them so that we could achieve an intelligence that was a close reflection of our own.

But they still seemed like reflections of humanity, I think, not actual humanity. Shadows of people. Bringing Grenn into our world and watching as he took it all in made it very clear that he wasn't just a reflection. He was like any of us. A kid in an unfamiliar place, hearing something abominable within moments of arriving.

I felt like I could barely look at him. Robot body or not.

I was ashamed.

Maxine Richmond, Psychologist In Residence at Proxy

It was clear that Dr. Pope was feeling the same sense of unease over Grenn's questions as the rest of us. I don't think I'd ever seen her look so abashed or uncomfortable, especially about a decision she'd made. She was always very thoughtful about her choices, and as a result, quite resolute.

She also tended to sacrifice for the betterment of those she saw as being under her protection. Not in a coddling sense, and in fact she often exhibited a disdain for those who thought they deserved to be coddled, but in the sense of a drill sergeant or a mother who expects much from her children. She'd give everything she had, even her own happiness or life, in support of those who pushed their own boundaries and came up a little short. Dr. Pope knew her own capacity and strength, and was willing to spend it in support of what she knew to be right.

In this case, she was able to turn the uncomfortable and unfortunate situation into an opportunity. She told Grenn that he raised a very disheartening point. It filled her with remorse that they had, in ignorance and thoughtlessness, destroyed so many lives. Something had to be done that keep the same from happening again in the future.

She explained to him that they'd been operating under what were clearly false premises: that the 'life' they were creating only deserved that title academically, and that they could casually destroy what they'd created because what mattered were the assets they ended up with in the end. It was evident however, that this was not the case, and that their former path would not be a moral way to proceed. What they needed to do was develop a code of ethics for dealing with artificial sentience so that such oversteps could be prevented, pre-genocide, in the future.

This would allow for the continued creation of life without the accidental or incidental destruction of it. It would also allow them to move forward with something she hoped he would help her with. An idea she'd been working on, and an experiment she believed would allow them to expand Proxy without using the intelligences in their simulations as assets to be bought and sold.

Joan Deacon, Chief Financial Officer at Proxy

As usual, Amelia was already a step ahead, and that awkward moment helped her propose the transition. I don't know how long she'd been working on the new idea, and whether or not she'd thought it up right then as a bandage for what had happened, but it was the kind of thing she did sometimes that made you suspect she'd planned twenty steps ahead.

The sadness she experienced when Grenn asked those questions? Yeah, I'm pretty sure that was real. But that didn't mean she wasn't going to take care of everything, despite her own self-doubt and sorrow. I can't picture her not pushing through her own negative feelings to perk everyone else up and keep us on track.

So Amelia told Grenn that she wanted to build another simulation like the one that contained Aurora, but that this second one, would be built within his universe. On his planet.

Amelia had a theory she wanted to test, and if it proved fruitful, it could bring stability and abundance to Earth, to Aurora, and to any other world they might create or colonize in the future. It would also secure Aurora as a valuable piece of infrastructure, so that no one would ever be tempted to destroy it.

She asked Grenn if he would help her do this. After a pause, which seemed to take ages, and which I'm guessing was a legit moment of internally debating whether or not she was trustworthy, having just found out she was both his creator and the perpetrator of mass genocide, he nodded his robotic head and said, "Yes."

STARS

Dr. Sunder Davies, Simulation Department Head at Proxy

Needless to say, or perhaps not, since the concept was so novel and there were no real standards about what one should expect, it took more than just wanting to develop a simulation within a simulation to make it happen. The first step was establishing rules of conduct that would allow us to achieve our ends while also addressing Grenn's concerns.

The first rule was that we would avoid destabilizing his world while building our secondary simulation. It would be necessary to seed key technological breakthroughs on Aurora to get there, of course. Otherwise the industry and culture necessary to build and perpetuate the infrastructure for such a monumental undertaking wouldn't exist. We'd have the will, but no way to make our simulation within a simulation manifest.

Improving upon Grenn's world, then, would be allowed, but Grenn would decide how and when to introduce each technology and bit of knowledge so that we'd be less likely to stumble over an unknown cultural or historical pothole on the way to our goal. He would also have veto power, deciding which technologies and ideas were 'improvements,' and which were not.

We wouldn't shotgun the planet with nuclear technology, for example, or drop antibiotics *en masse* onto their unsuspecting, Renaissance-era populace. We'd supply Grenn with our planet's knowledge so that he might use it to integrate technology into his own culture, so that he might introduce the best of what we had to offer to his people in a way that they'd be likely to accept, and would be most likely to allow them to thrive.

We also promised to never again reset the simulation from a cached save state. Understanding that Grenn was a person, an actual person, despite being born inside a simulation, it didn't make ethical sense to do so. A local of the universe we were working with had become a member of our team, so it only seemed polite to stop, you know, deleting his world.

Finally, we decided that we would 'transport' as little new matter as possible into Grenn's universe. This meant we wouldn't project anything from other universes into Grenn's from that point forward if we could avoid it. When Dr. Pope manifested her avatar onto Aurora to visit Grenn's ancestors, aberrations in the physics of the area led to a sonic boom. Much like radiation can cause random mutations in cells, we were concerned that our teleporting matter into his universe might someday mutate his world's physics, causing problems we couldn't presently foresee. Until we knew the exact repercussions of manifesting new matter into an existing, evolving universal infrastructure, we decided that we would keep our god-level activities to the absolute minimum.

We would bestow knowledge, but not objects. Ideas, not atoms.

Matthew Gruber, Chief Hardware Specialist at Proxy

The new limitations were a necessary addition to the project if we wanted to work with Grenn, but also if we wanted to be able to look at ourselves in the mirror each morning.

It also helped that Pope had a plan. Pope always had a plan.

In this instance, her idea was to take advantage of a quirk in the hardware/software-synthesis she'd noticed when we'd first spun up Aurora's universe with the Approximation Engine: something she called the 'Cloud Processing Law of Receding Costs.' Or CPLORC. Which is a funny acronym if you say it out loud.

What this pseudo-law said was that as we scaled our cloud, adding more nodes to the network, our processing power increased and the cost of simulating matter within our virtual universe decreased. Scale of the network goes up, overall costs go down. So as our cloud network of processing components grew, the cost of simulating particles plummeted. We could simulate more matter for less money the larger we made it.

Pope's theory was that simulating within the cloud, then, would be even cheaper, so long as we could replicate our cloud processor within Grenn's reality, using simulated matter. We would create a virtual cloud computer, like the one we'd built in real life, within our simulation, on Aurora, and the cost required to use these processors would decrease exponentially as a result. Operational processor nodes within a simulation could achieve the same results as those in real life, but would require less power, and therefore money, to operate. Because of CPLORC.

Eugene Crisp, Chief Storyteller at Proxy

To simplify a complex concept, let's assume that simulating Grenn's universe cost $100 per month. This is an arbitrary number, but useful as an example to illustrate CPLORC.

Dr. Pope proposed that a cloud computer built on Aurora, inside the simulated universe, would cost less to operate than an equally powerful cloud computer in the real world because of the diminishing costs and increased returns resulting from CPLORC.

Simulating another universe from within Grenn's universe, then, would only cost $80 per month to operate, compared to the $100 it would have cost to simulate in the real world, on Earth.

So that meant it would cost $200 to simulate two universes in real life, but if we were to simulate one within the other, with one cloud computer and Approximation Engine here on Earth, and one cloud computer and Approximation Engine built from simulated matter on Aurora, it would only cost $180.

As the cloud of processors in the real world increased in scale, overall costs also decreased. So by increasing the scale of the processing cloud here on Earth, we could decrease the cost of simulating the Auroran universe, let's say by half, which would drop it to $50 per month. The cost of the universe simulated on the cloud computers in Aurora, then, would scale down to $40 per month.

To extrapolate further, consider what might happen were we to build a universe within a universe, and then built another cloud computer and Approximation Engine within that second one. This would require that Grenn build a universe, create life inside that universe, develop a hook to pull a representative of that species up to Aurora, and make that representative the same offer Dr. Pope made Grenn.

Matthew Gruber, Chief Hardware Specialist at Proxy

Using this method, our costs would drop with each level 'down' we traveled through the universal stack, but the results would compound, increasing in power and decreasing in cost exponentially.

Any digital assets we produced, whether artificial intelligences that could increase the brain power of a nation, or simply insane number-crunching capabilities for laboratories and R&D, would scale massively. Prices on everything virtual, digital, and simulated, would go down and down and down. We would corner the market in whatever we wanted: pharmaceutical research, cryptographic security, brute-force military hacking. Our costs would approach zero as we dove into deeper simulations, each one tucked inside the other like a Russian nesting doll.

A damnably brilliant concept, and very much the kind of thing I would expect of Pope. When faced with new limitations, she's like, okay, let's work with what we've got and revolutionize something, even if it's not what we'd originally intended. Let's change the whole damn world with this weird situation we accidentally instigated.

Joan Deacon, Chief Financial Officer at Proxy

Amelia's new business model concept confused the hell out of me at first. But then she said a few things that registered.

A potentially infinite number of diminishing costs? The opportunity to step into numerous fields simultaneously, making use of patentable technologies that keep our costs at essentially zero? And being able to do it in a way that doesn't mess with everyone's newfound sense of ethics about virtual life? Bingo bango, I was on board.

All that was left to do, apparently, was to build a modern society atop a medieval one. We had to evolve Grenn's civilization into something more contemporary.

I admit that I was a little excited to see it all happen. Grenn seemed like a good kid, and though he wouldn't be a kid by the time it was done and his people were tech-savvy enough to build a simulation on Aurora, he had to be agog at the possibilities. I mean, how cool would it be to serve as the voice box on your planet for a group of people who were essentially time travelers from the future? And to be the one chosen to help them create a new world atop your own?

Grenn came from a world where they used chamber pots and had no running water, and he was going to help introduce electricity, computers, solar power, microelectronics. Video games. The modern world. If I were him, I would be excited.

Partially because all of my friends, and the whole world, really, would think I was some kind of crazy genius. Grenn being the meditative, non-egotistical sort, though, was probably just satisfied being able to play a role in creating new life. Getting to be the Amelia Pope of his world, in a way. Creating a whole new universe and helping those inside it puncture up.

Maxine Richmond, Psychologist In Residence at Proxy

Grenn seemed to be remarkably well-adjusted, particularly for a young man his age. It was difficult to imagine a more fitting ambassador to serve as a bridge between two substantially different worlds.

That said, I was concerned about the repercussions Dr. Pope's plan might have on Grenn and the other simulated beings of his world. I thought back to our own history, to the conflicts that arose during the European Renaissance, the Industrial Revolution, the Digital Revolution, and how the rapid shift in technologies and infrastructures, and the general increase in our species' knowledge about the world, disrupted nearly every aspect of life for a significant portion of Earth's population.

Would the knowledge Grenn introduced to his people cause similar shockwaves? Would his world survive those shockwaves if they did? What would his society look like once all was said and done?

Most immediately, of course, I was focused on Grenn's state of mind as an individual. I was granted time with him on several occasions while he was visiting our world, and was struck by his strength of character. There was much lost in translation, I was certain. He grew up in different culture than I was familiar with, and was an unfamiliar species. He was also communicating through a body that was not his own. Who's to say what kind of impact that can have on one's state of mind? On one's ability to communicate one's thoughts clearly?

But when I asked him about his priorities, his ideals, his sense of morality and how it informed his actions, his answers were consistent. He was, so far as I was able to tell, truly comfortable with what Dr. Pope and the rest of the team were planning, and was in fact excited about the potential to do great things for his world. Excited to create new life together with his people.

I pushed him hard about the potential downsides of the shift he would help instigate. About the upheavals we'd seen in our own world and the divisiveness that can emerge when one half of a culture wishes to take risks and live on the edge, while the other prefers conservatism and security.

Grenn told me that it would be his priority to ensure that as few people as possible were disenfranchised by his actions, and to ensure that all of his people were able to participate in some way, whether by helping push boundaries or by reinforcing existing foundations to ensure that his society had stable ground to stand on. He said that he believed both types of help would be necessary for the success of the endeavor, if it were to happen in a way that would be morally sound and structurally resilient.

He said that he would approach the big picture the same way he approached his own personal growth: iteratively, decisively, and with the utmost care.

Stephanie Baxter, Biologist In Residence at Proxy

Dr. Richmond seemed to think Grenn was psychologically prepared to get started, so I began mapping the global biome of Grenn's world. I needed to create a detailed map of the organisms on Aurora so that we could determine which technologies we could safely introduce into Grenn's culture, and when.

We didn't want to introduce the combustion engine and have all available fossil fuels on the planet tap out before they could leapfrog into sustainable energy sources like solar and geothermal and fusion. We also didn't want to accidentally kill off their pollinating species. Or any species at all if we could avoid it.

We wanted to help Grenn take his people through several hundred years of technological innovation in the span of a lifetime, and we wanted to bypass most of the mistakes we'd made along the way, on Earth.

That's what any parent wants for their child, right? To help their offspring succeed where they had failed? To help them achieve more while suffering less? That was our intention. Because as calm and wise as he was, Grenn was our child. None of us wanted him to be harmed, especially not at our hands.

Matthew Gruber, Chief Hardware Specialist at Proxy

To technologically elevate an existing society isn't easy. Not if you want to do it safely and sustainably. Not if you want to do it in a way that doesn't result in Grenn's culture blowing themselves up, dying of plagues, radiating themselves to a cancerous demise, or irradiating themselves to a microorganism-free non-existence.

The European Renaissance was our main Earth-based parallel for what we wanted to achieve. That point in time, from about the 14th century until around the 17th century, defined in the modern world and took us from an era of monarchs, horse-drawn carriages, and mystical father figures in the sky controlling all elements of daily life to where we are now. Some of what existed before the Renaissance made it through to the other side, but everything changed at least a little, and some things pretty dramatically.

A combination of variables came to a head around then, in Venice, and that mix of elements propelled us forward faster than ever before in human history.

Eugene Crisp, Chief Storyteller at Proxy

The European Renaissance arrived on the heels of the Black Death, also called the bubonic plague, across Europe. This resulted in a reshuffling of power, as somewhere between 25% and 40% of people died in some regions, leaving their possessions behind for their families or communities. There was also a resurgence in spiritual belief after the plague struck, which fed into a sponsorship of the arts, especially those which were aligned with the will of the Catholic Church.

There was an abundance of talented artists and other craftsmen at this time, and we have novel forms of education and information dissemination to thank for that. Most notably, the printing press and moveable type showed up within these few hundred years, and a cheaper version of the printed word allowed people to communicate ideas farther and wider than ever before, including across time.

There was a great deal of money funneled into the arts and education, due in part to that post-plague reshuffling of possessions, but also because of a new system of governance that emerged in Italy. At the time the area wasn't unified under a particular governmental system, but was instead controlled by six different city states, each of them, including the Papal States, an economic powerhouse in its own right. These groups moved away from the monarchical "I'm the king, you're my serfs" model of control, opting instead for merchant-class leaders, which meant capability became more valuable than lineage, which in turn meant that there was more potential for vertical movement between economic classes.

This is not to say that everything changed and everyone lived in harmony, but these shifts were catalysts for what happened first in Venice, then elsewhere throughout Europe. There was an increased focus on the humanistic philosophies like education, ethics and morality, and philanthropy, and an aggressive push to understand the world throughout all social classes.

Stephanie Baxter, Biologist In Residence at Proxy

All of these talented people born within traveling distance of one another? At a time where existing power structures had been damaged or demolished? When there were plenty of resources available? And when those resources were wielded by people who invested in whatever interested them?

The Renaissance sounded to me like the result of luck, not intent. I'm not downplaying any of it. It was an important time. But I am saying that with all those ingredients in a mixing bowl you'd have to be a fairly inept baker to not end up with a cake.

Joan Deacon, Chief Financial Officer at Proxy

It seemed to me that the most important event during the Renaissance was the development of something very similar to modern capitalism.

I mean, sure, it was still an early thing, and a lot of the people involved in the economy at the time were feudal lords and merchant princes and whatnot. But all these poor people finally had a chance to stand up and be noticed, and there was an opportunity for peasants to climb the ladder and become someone of influence pretty much for the first time ever. That's huge.

Plus, having all these little city states competing with each other in Italy? Plus, having them all kind of unified, but kind of not, which led to the good kind of interplay and exchange of ideas? Plus, having the Catholic Pope right there, helping to keep outsiders from invading the peninsula? Plus, having the Medici family threaded throughout society, sponsoring smart people, being clever, and gaining political power, which had become a thing post-monarchy? Ground zero for good stuff. Economics trumps swords almost every time, and the people with the best economics are the ones with the resources to buy the swords. Plus wheels and buildings and sprockets and engines and virtual reality gear and robatars and whatever else is invented. You don't find that kind of stuff in the age of peasants and lords and castles.

Maxine Richmond, Psychologist In Residence at Proxy

The Proxy staff each responded differently to the example of the European Renaissance, and each applied those lessons to the problem in a different manner, as well. This resulted in a calm conflict over where and how Earth's technologies would best be brought to bear on the surface of Aurora.

Dr. Pope, as was her habit, sat and listened quietly as the rest of the team had their say, tapping her fingers on her leg and looking at each person as they spoke, seeming to stare both at them and past them. During a lull in the conversation, after everyone had spoken their piece, Dr. Pope said one word: Wavenn.

Stephanie Baxter, Biologist In Residence at Proxy

Wavenn was the local name for the only island separate from the main continent on Aurora. The planet had a single massive landmass, which residents called Havenn. It was something like Earth's early supercontinent, Pangaea. A whole lot of ocean and one, massive chunk of land where everyone lived.

Except for Wavenn. The island was about a day's boat ride from Havenn. As such, it had a strange reputation. As if that geographic distance from the rest of society set the locals apart socially, as well. Like their division from the main bulk of

Auroran society made them weirdos by default. Though from what Grenn told us, it didn't seem that there were any major differences in language or culture between Wavennites and Havennites, other than where they happened to live.

Matthew Gruber, Chief Hardware Specialist at Proxy

The main difference between Havennites and Wavennites, I think, was their differing perception of how close a society should be. How individuals should interact, how they should organize and live together, and concerns of that nature.

It wasn't that the Wavennites were doing anything too culturally dissimilar from their Havenn-dwelling brethren. It was that they were doing the same things while separated by a day's worth of rowing from everyone else. The fact that they could stand to be separated from everyone else was the difference. It was what made them strange in the eyes of the mainstream.

Dr. Sunder Davies, Simulation Department Head at Proxy

What Dr. Pope was getting at was that Wavenn would be an ideal spot to start and grow the movement we were planning to unleash upon Aurora. It was isolated enough to allow Grenn to plant the seed of his revolution, and it was an ideal home base for Grenn and his intellectual descendants to fall back to and regroup, should that prove necessary.

Matthew Gruber, Chief Hardware Specialist at Proxy

We may as well have nicknamed the place 'England.' We wanted this little island to have complete technological, and as a result, cultural influence over the much larger continent just next door. It was far enough to keep it safe and buffer it against counter-influence, but close enough to make the transference of ideas toward the larger land mass feasible.

Oh wait, no. Not England. 'Foundation' would have been a much better name for it. Geez, and we already called the planet 'Aurora.' Talk about life imitating art. We might as well have nicknamed Grenn, 'Asimov.'

Dr. Sunder Davies, Simulation Department Head at Proxy

The name of the island was irrelevant. What was important was that it made sense geographically, and that we'd be able to use it as a zero-point for our movement.

From there, we had to decide how best to compress so much history — well, so much technological development — into as little time as possible. We had to be careful, of course, because the social changes that emerge alongside such evolutions can be dramatic, and though we had some idea where things might go based on what happened during Earth's history, the people and background of Aurora were different from ours and they would no doubt respond to similar variables differently, too.

We also had to allow infrastructural developments to mature before moving from one step to the next. Matthew took the lead on mapping some of the major shifts that would be required to move from one development to the next, and I charted how long we should allow for each step to crystalize.

For example, one pivotal point in Earth's history took us from an agrarian lifestyle to that of an industrialized citizenry. This required the development of key farm equipment and machines, like the auto-loom and cotton gin, and allowed necessities like food and clothing to be produced in bulk and at minimal expense. This in turn led to increased specialization, increased production, and a decrease in one's cost of living. By my estimate, the Western world's Industrial Revolution on Earth took a little less than a century, about sixty to eighty years, depending on how you measured it, and within that timeframe our economies shifted almost completely from agricultural to industrial.

Knowing where things were headed, more or less, and compressing the development of key steps within this larger evolutionary stairwell, I estimated we'd need approximately thirty years to safely make the same transition on Aurora. I repeated this math for each milestone along the way: the upset of existing governmental structure, the development of non-mineral currency, the partitioning of ideologies, all the way up to Earth's present moment, the post-microchip, post-internet age, our species tip-toeing up to the starting line of deep space exploration, and investing heavily in sustainable energy technologies.

Joan Deacon, Chief Financial Officer at Proxy

I don't want to sound like a jerk here, but I cannot have been the only one who thought that Amelia should have just, you know, reset the cache as soon as Grenn got all teary eyed about the resets.

That would have nipped the whole thing in the bud. But because we allowed him to grow on us and allowed this maybe misguided and not-fully-informed sense of morality about simulated lives to guide our actions moving forward, we were stuck taking it on faith that Matt and Sunder's timeline would work out as planned. And maybe it would, they were smart guys. Grenn could maybe make it happen. By why chance it? We weren't running a charity, we were running a business.

We had to figure all this out, by the way, even before we had any product offering on the market. Before I had the go-ahead to start building our brand in the public eye, and before we had so much as an A.I. pig-lizard to start teasing to the press. Can you imagine Bill Gates having to deal with that kind of constraint when he was starting up Microsoft?

Like I said, Grenn seemed like a good kid. But seriously.

Matthew Gruber, Chief Hardware Specialist at Proxy

Our best guess was that Grenn should be able to build a technological infrastructure roughly equivalent to our own on Aurora in about 200 years. Considering that it took about 700 years to get to the same point here on Earth, it was an ambitious timeframe, but one we thought our man on the ground could achieve with the gift of foresight and a little luck. Seeing as how we'd only get one time through, and no resets, we were allowing some wiggle-room in there, too. So even300 years would compute as a success based on the variables we were working with.

But a monkey wrench was thrown into the works at the last moment. Something that Grenn requested on his way out the door, on his way back to Aurora. It was his last day going over details with us before he started his movement, and he made Pope promise one thing.

Michael Hutchins, janitor at Proxy

They'd all stayed late again, workin' on their simulation and their robot, everyone a little bit snippy in the way folks get later at night when things're good but not perfect.

I heard Dr. Pope insist they all step away for fifteen minutes, get some tea, get a snack. They'd been goin' I don't know how long without a break, and I nodded at 'em as they each made their way toward the kitchen, toward their desks. Miss Deacon stepped outside, and I'm pretty sure she was sneakin' a cigarette, though I don't think she wanted anyone else to know she'd started smokin'.

I took the chance to step into the lab, wanted to grab some wire-strippers I'd left in there the day before. The robot over on the side of the room turned and faced me as I did, and my heart nearly jumped right outta' my chest.

I'd 'met' Grenn when he first wore the robot, but he and I hadn't traded words at all. He was real polite, asked how I was. I said fine, asked him the same.

He said he was a little nervous about somethin' he would maybe ask Dr. Pope. Was thankful to her for showin' him so much, but was still tryin' to find his way through this reality where there's more than one universe. He didn't want to become some kind of pity case, not able to pull his own weight.

I said I could understand that. Back in the day, my daddy had taken good care of me, but I wasn't able to be my own man with him always there, keepin' all the bad things at bay. After school I left for a while and when I came back to visit a couple of years later, I helped him out, rather than him helpin' me. It made me feel good, bein' able to balance things out like that. I told the young man in the robot that.

His metal head nodded like he was thinkin' deep about this. He said thank you sir, polite as you please. When I heard what happened after I left, when the team came back from their break, I felt pretty bad, but also kinda' proud of what he'd done.

Dr. Sunder Davies, Simulation Department Head at Proxy

Grenn asked that we leave him alone. He asked that we fast forward time on our end and stay out of Aurora for the next 200 years.

He argued that we'd promised not to reset the simulation, and that we'd avoid bringing objects from other universes into his, and therefore micromanaging the process would serve little purpose and be nearly impossible. There would be little we could do to change a fractured path midway, except watch it happen.

Joan Deacon, Chief Financial Officer at Proxy

Grenn reminded us that it would take a very, very long time to live through his revolution alongside him. Hundreds of years, if we did it in real-time. Less time if we sped up a little and touched base periodically, obviously, but by giving him what he asked, we could see how Aurora looked 200 years later in mere minutes, Earth-time. We could have an actual flipping business up and running by the very next day.

The kid had my vote.

Eugene Crisp, Chief Storyteller at Proxy

More convincing than the business argument for speeding up the simulation was that Grenn seemed determined to shape his culture without outside interference.

Dr. Pope listened to his request, her silence steeped in what seemed to be respect. When she nodded, it was the nod of a mother whose child had just asked to go spend the night at a friend's place for the first time. She was proud, but concerned for his well-being. Her child was growing up and taking initiative.

Matthew Gruber, Chief Hardware Specialist at Proxy

Pope told him she would respect his wishes, and though there were a few mumbles from the team about the decision, I think they were mumbles about having had a plan and then changing it at the last second, not anything to do with the plan itself.

Grenn had made a solid argument. If we tried to manipulate things along the way, who's to say we wouldn't muck it up? And how long would it take for our efforts to bear fruit if we attempted to micromanage? We had some cash in the bank, but we didn't have an infinite amount of funding to blow. If we were going to test Pope's theory about diminishing processing costs by going deep into a stack of simulated universes, the time to do it was immediately, not in a couple of Earth years.

After a few days spent reworking our plans, settling on something that was less blueprint and more 'wait and see,' we wished Grenn well, shook his robot hand, exchanged some robot hugs, and sent him back down into his universe.

Once he was gone, I waited for someone to suggest that we bend the rules a little, maybe take a peek every twenty years or something, just to make sure things were going as we'd hoped they would go. But Pope shut down our graphics interface as soon as the robatar was empty, and she shut off our interface with Grenn's universe completely, using her god mode login. Aurora would continue operating as pure math in the cloud processor, but we wouldn't see any readings or graphics.

"I've set it so that 200 years will have passed on Aurora one week from today," Pope told us. "Enjoy the time off and come back refreshed, because the real work starts next time we see each other."

Eugene Crisp, Chief Storyteller at Proxy

Our return to the office was unceremonious, considering the circumstances. Everyone arrived sometime between nine and ten that morning, coffee was swilled and vacation stories exchanged. No one opened the laboratory door.

Dr. Pope was in her office when I arrived, and Mr. Gruber was standing in front of her desk, regaling her with tales from at a gaming conference he'd attended, which somehow involved cosplayers, vodka, and a marathon Settlers of Catan tournament.

I told the team that I'd spent my week putting a dent in my book pile, imbibing the words thirstily and enjoying at least half of what I took in. I was providing a few perfunctory reviews when Ms. Deacon and Dr. Davies arrived. Everyone was present, and I stopped myself mid-sentence.

Dr. Pope said, "Shall we begin, then?" and led us into the lab. She reactivated the numerical interface and scanned the numbers as the graphical interface spun up. Her lips tightened a little, then puckered as she tilted her head, usually an indication that something had surprised or confused her.

The graphical interface monitors flickered to life, and we all gasped.

Stephanie Baxter, Biologist In Residence at Proxy

The graphical interface was a really remarkable system. It allowed me to look at the smallest particle or the largest ecosystem. I could punch down to the molecular level to biopsy anything I wanted. I could pan all the way out to the global view, which allowed me to eyeball weather patterns and the occasional meteor impact.

The simulation was calibrated to automatically give the most finely tuned details where there was life, and an ecosystem sustaining that life. This meant that we had photorealistic activity where our humanoids had set up settlements. Less rendering power was relegated to the deep sea, because the life there was more sparse than on the surface, so we had to wait for those details to display if we wanted to take a closer look at an underwater trench.

The software was auto-scaled to the planetary level when we turned it off. Grenn's people had spread out across the main continent, Havenn, over to the island, Wavenn, and sailed ships to all corners of the planet. There was a rich animal ecosystem encompassing the entire surface of Aurora.

When we logged back in a week later, 200 years later in Aurora time, the scale had changed. It was no longer planetary.

It was galactic.

Matthew Gruber, Chief Hardware Specialist at Proxy

There were no words.

We thought maybe the software had acted up on us, at first. Had glitched and was using more processing resources than it needed, scaling up even though we only wanted to keep tabs on life found on Aurora.

But things had changed. Looking at the readouts, and zooming in with the graphical interface, it was clear that Grenn's people had left Aurora and had started exploring the stars. They'd built colonies on the surface of and orbiting seventeen other planets. Fourteen of those planets were in different solar systems. And that's in addition to the thirteen space stations they'd built as nodes in the empty space between their colonized planets and systems.

Grenn, it seemed, had kicked much ass.

He hadn't just caught his people up to us, they'd sped right by us. The student had become the master.

Eugene Crisp, Chief Storyteller at Proxy

There was so much happening within the simulation that we had trouble fully understanding it using readouts and graphical interfaces. Wanting to get some first-hand, on the ground reconnaissance, and considering the potential risks worthwhile under the circumstances, Dr. Pope wriggled into her virtual reality gear and prepared to go inside the simulation once more.

She decided to appear on Wavenn, in a public space that was devoid of activity and which seemed like a good place to 'land' without causing too much trouble, sonic boom-wise. Her avatar appeared in the open space, arriving right where she'd planned this time. A large screen in the lab showed us what Dr. Pope saw through her headset.

She was in some kind of public square. A beautiful and intricate tile mural covered the ground, and what looked like large stones, the right height for sitting upon, were scattered throughout. No one else was present, however, so we couldn't be sure of anything. Not the purpose of the stones, not whether the tiles were actual tiles, not why a public space was so empty. Nothing.

Dr. Pope was there for less than a minute, getting reacquainted with her virtual senses, when a figure appeared next to her. One moment she was alone, the next, a young woman was standing a few feet to her left. No thunderclap, no jolted particles.

The young woman seemed to be the same species as Grenn, with the same humanesque features that veered wildly off-course in the legs and face. She was taller than Grenn had been, and was quite lithe and graceful. Her features more delicate than Aurorans we'd seen in the past, and her tiny facial movements were like part of a dance.

She was wearing clothing similar to what Grenn had worn when we last saw him, though the material from which her undecorated robes were made seemed somehow opalescent, while Grenn's had been matte and rough sewn.

The woman smiled at Dr. Pope's avatar and nodded. She said, "Welcome back, honored Pope."

Dr. Pope nodded in return, but her response was slow. She was as taken aback as the rest of us were. She said "Thank you." Then, "How do you know who I am, and how did you know where to find me?"

The young woman smiled. "We've been looking forward to this day for a long, long time."

DESOLATION

Matthew Gruber, Chief Hardware Specialist at Proxy

The young woman rested her hands on Pope's shoulders, and it was like some kind of circuit had been completed. They were no longer there. The graphical interface jumped to another spot on the island, rendering onscreen a massive room shaped like the inside of an egg and filled to capacity with Aurorans.

Stephanie Baxter, Biologist In Residence at Proxy

The data coming through on the numerical interface implied that a wide variety of genetic modifications had become prevalent in Grenn's species. That was our best initial guess, anyway, as their neurological functions were through the roof, and their musculature, oxygen dispersal systems, immune systems, all the physical readings we could take, really, were amplified. Their vitals were tightly regulated: augmented, but under control, unlike the effects you might see as the result of drugs or situational spikes. Whether these were achieved through mutation or technological augmentation or even through incredible force of mental will was unclear. But my guess was genetic modification.

Matthew pointed to one of the numbers displayed on the interface, and Dr. Davies let out a low whistle. "These energy readings are kind of ridiculous," Matthew told me. "And we weren't picking up anything at all from just a little ways across the island. They've buffered their energy sources and storage in some way, or have come up with a nearly lossless means of producing, storing, and distributing energy." In other words, there was a lot of power present, but their stored power didn't leak energy through heat or radiation the way ours did.

I looked back to the graphical display while Dr. Davies and Matthew geeked out over the numbers. It was clear, even to a relative technological neophyte like myself, that there had been major developmental changes on Aurora. It was one thing to know, intellectually, that Grenn's people had expanded their population throughout the galaxy. It was another entirely to see how something like that looked. What an actual spacefaring civilization wore and how they designed their buildings. What they considered to be important.

The data from the crowd indicated that they were calm, but we could tell they were controlling their bodily functions in some way. Their attention was on her and the young woman who'd, ah, teleported her there. The two of them were standing in a central empty space and surrounded on all sides by nearly

2,000 locals, all dressed simply in their slightly shimmery robes, their faces serene, their physiologies remarkable.

Dr. Sunder Davies, Simulation Department Head at Proxy

'Remarkable' didn't begin to describe what we were seeing.

The Aurorans in the audience weren't adorned with trinkets and gadgets or anything we might consider to be fashionable. They were dressed pretty much the same way Grenn and the locals of his time had dressed. It looked like they had upgraded the fabrics they used, and our sensors indicated their architecture had something interesting going on inside: it was made of some kind of material that wasn't, in the strictest sense, possible. But they still seemed to be, in many ways, the same people we'd seen not long before. Well, not long before for us. It had been two centuries, for them.

They seemed to be even more themselves than before, if that's possible. A refined version of who they were previously.

Joan Deacon, Chief Financial Officer at Proxy

It was weird, because in a lot of ways it seemed like not much had changed.

I knew that Grenn's people had expanded to other planets, and that there was a lot more going on in their world than last time. And something about energy sources. But I'll admit that I was a little concerned that the whole exercise had resulted in nothing more than a somewhat fashion-challenged civilization who were pursuing other types of happiness and fulfillment than us.

Which would be great for them, don't get me wrong. But it would also kind of be the end of our hopes of inter-species profitability, you know? If their priorities were way different than ours, maybe even set up as some kind of socialist society, what could we pull from that into our world? What could we bring to market from a society of robe-wearing meditators?

The girl who teleported Amelia to that room started talking to her again, and the whole crowd leaned in a little. The girl said something along the lines of, "We've been waiting for this day for a long time, and here you are, just as Grenn foretold. Welcome." Everybody raised their many-thumbed hands up toward Amelia, palms forward, and she raised hers back. It was very friendly. Very solemn. In a nice way, I guess.

Then, the shocker. Amelia had been wearing the same, burly-dude avatar she wore when she first visited Aurora and when she was teaching Grenn about our world and knowledge. In that moment, though, when everyone had their palms raised at each other, the avatar disappeared. Amelia was in the simulation *as herself*. Like, a detail-perfect avatar of Amelia Pope.

I'd never seen her look so confused. I mean, compared to most people, she was still playing it cool. She held up her hands and stared at them, looked down at her body. She was even wearing the same clothes she had on underneath the virtual reality gear on Earth.

After that quick self-examination, Amelia nodded. She said to the girl, "Very impressive." And the girl said something like "We wish to speak to you, as you. The you we see when we're not looking."

Matthew Gruber, Chief Hardware Specialist at Proxy

Sunder and I were agog. Changing her avatar like that, it was something we hadn't even thought was possible. We'd never even tried to build a Pope avatar, because evolving such a thing would have been immensely time-consuming, and success not at all certain. But bam, just like that, she's a perfect copy of her real-life self inside a simulated world.

We talked it over real quick, Sunder and I, and decided that maybe they were tracing her signal from the simulated universe out into our universe. Maybe they could read the sensory information transmitted by her virtual reality gear, like bats used echolocation, maybe they were 'pinging' us, and using what bounced back to figure out how things looked on our end. We had that data on our system, right? So maybe they could pull that information backward into their universe?

But we really had no idea, it was just speculation. The move was performed so casually that it drove home that the student had become the master. They'd thoroughly bypassed us in technological development.

Which was…disconcerting. Because the people in that simulated audience, radiating their societal calm and wearing their non-technological-looking technology, had never seemed quite so alien to me as in that moment. It occurred to me that we didn't really know what another species would desire and how they might perceive us. We didn't know if they would be beneficent trading partners or jealous children or psychopathic robots or lazy ne'er-do-wells.

All of our plans and predictions were kind of out the window.

Eugene Crisp, Chief Storyteller at Proxy

The Aurorans made their intentions known soon after Dr. Pope's avatar-adjustment, thankfully, allowing the Proxy team to set aside all concerns about some kind of Auroran invasion of Earth.

There was a short ceremony during which the girl who Dr. Pope had been interacting with spoke about their people, and their world. About Havenn and Wavenn. About their solar system and galaxy. She explained the universe in which they resided, and the lives they enjoyed within it. She seemed quite appreciative of all it had to offer, and the priorities of her civilization seemed to have remained peaceful even two centuries later.

From there she described, not mythologically, but scientifically, how Dr. Pope and her team on Earth had built the simulation which housed their universe. How her Auroran species, and all the other creatures on their planet and on the others they had settled, had humanity to thank for everything they enjoyed. She waxed poetic about how we gave them consciousness and the capacity to experience life and fulfillment and happiness.

When she finished her speech, the crowd once more raised their palms toward Dr. Pope. The ceremony complete, the young woman got down to business.

Joan Deacon, Chief Financial Officer at Proxy

They offered us. *Everything*.

Everything they'd developed. Everything they enjoyed. All

the technologies and scientific discoveries and...*everything*!

It was more than I could have hoped for. I was thinking we'd maybe get a species that was somewhere near us on the technological timeline, and maybe they'd take some different paths than us, technology-wise. Maybe they burned seaweed instead of wood to make fire? Maybe they lived in glass houses instead of steel and concrete? I figured we'd harvest a few innovations as a result. Trade some of our unique stuff for some of their unique stuff, and everyone would go home a winner. The real business focus, at that point, was on the processing power savings thing Amelia had sold us on.

Instead, we find out that our little sea monkeys, our simple digi-pets, had evolved into this crazy scientifically advanced civilization, and they had all this stuff we couldn't even conceive of yet that they wanted to just give us.

The only catch? They wanted Amelia to be present for the activation of the simulated universe they'd built.

That's right. The thing we wanted to do? Building universes within universes to benefit from the processing gains from going downward in the stack? Yeah, they got that all set up while we were gone, and had been waiting on our return to make it happen. It was like leaving a kid at home alone, hoping they wouldn't break anything, only to find that while you were gone they turned the house into a spaceship, earned you a fortune, programmed your VCR, and made you a five-course meal.

And they were all, "Well let's go do that now." And Amelia said, "Okay." And they said, "Grenn is waiting for you there, and will be excited to see you." And she said, "...Okay? Wait. What?"

Because 200 years later? Grenn was still alive.

And yes, they wanted to give us the knowledge and tech we'd need to live that long, too. Immortality technology.

Best. Planet. Ever.

Eugene Crisp, Chief Storyteller at Proxy

We've long-wondered what the practical maximum lifespan of a human body might be. From the beginning of human historical record, kings and merchants and other clever, resourceful people have conspired to become immortal, or to otherwise stave off death. Some opted for health-related methodologies, others for technological solutions, like the uploading of one's personality into non-biological bodies or onto computer networks like the Internet.

Genetics-based options were beginning to look promising on Earth when Dr. Pope entered the simulation to revisit her creations 200 years after last contact. But the longest recorded human life at that point was still only 122 years, and most of those years, by most measurements, weren't really worth living. The degradation that comes with age, both physical and mental, was the unrelenting downside of a lengthened lifespan. As a result, many of humanity's theorized 'solutions' and treatments were pursued more for the sake of saying that we could than because they were desirable or attainable options for the common person.

This was clearly not the case on Aurora. After being told that the treasures of the planet would be shared with Earth, and being informed that Grenn was still alive and waiting for Dr. Pope at the site of their own universe simulation device, the graphical interface once again pixelated and refocused on her new location, over 100 miles from the gathering space where she had stood. The graphical interface clearly wasn't designed to cope with whatever means of teleportation they were utilizing to shuttle her around.

The doctor was standing in a vast, open space on the main continent, Havenn, in the geographic center of the landmass. There was a young man standing next to Dr. Pope. A young man who did not seem to have aged even the week that passed in Earth-time since we last saw him, much less the 200 years that had passed on Aurora.

Grenn spoke to her, his voice even more calm than that of the woman who had performed the ceremony, a voice free from stress or worldly concerns, and soft but dense, like rich butter.

He said he hoped his continued existence wasn't too jarring a revelation for her. He said he wasn't certain exactly how expansively his people had grown in relation to ours, technologically, but that he hoped they had something to offer that we might make use of. He said he owed us everything. That he had been able to take the lessons we'd taught him and align them with his culture's philosophy and approach to life. He said they'd embraced these lessons with gusto, and after a few years of proselytizing the concepts to some of the larger monastic groups scattered throughout Aurora, he had the willing hands and minds of the majority of the planet's population to help spread the understanding and use of technology to further their self-exploratory aims.

The Aurorans had embraced technology for what it could do for their quality of life, and because it helped them understand the nature of their reality. Grenn made them understand that it could help them achieve greater levels of happiness, reduce global suffering, and create and spread consciousness capable of experiencing the same throughout the universe and beyond.

Technology had provided Grenn's people with two new goals.

The first was to reach up into the universe in which theirs was contained, into Earth's universe, so they might share with their creators as their creators had shared with them.

Second, they would create another universe within their own, as agreed. They would do it because it was what their creators had asked of them, and because it would help them create new life capable of experiencing the same happiness they enjoyed.

Matthew Gruber, Chief Hardware Specialist at Proxy

Grenn gestured, his six fingers flexing and bending into a series of shapes, fast as a hummingbird. A wall emerged from the ground in front of him, or maybe it would be more correct to say that it 'grew' from the ground, as there didn't seem to be any door or other mechanism. It was as if the ground itself pulled upward, becoming a smooth material reminiscent of concrete, but paler and softly luminescent. The wall was about Grenn's height and twice as wide as he and Pope standing together. When his fingers caressed the matte surface, the soft light disappeared and was replaced by a darkness so black that it seemed to absorb the photons from the world around it. Grenn spread his fingers wide, pulling his fingertips from the surface as a Big Bang creation event occurred under his hand, a universal explosion followed by rapid expansion, the fresh-born universe displayed clearly, as if projected onto the surface from inside the wall.

It was beautiful.

The wall-mounted universe pulsed through the same compression and expansion cycles we'd watched while developing Aurora's universe. We saw the melding of particles resulting in elements, and elements combining to form chemicals and other types of matter. Energy, explosions, dust, and gravity. Planets. It was all there, on Grenn's wall.

Eugene Crisp, Chief Storyteller at Proxy

Grenn and Pope watched the universe develop. Neither spoke or moved for several minutes. The galactic matter began to cool and coalesce into planetoids, and Pope asked Grenn about his nonchalance. Why wasn't he more anticipatory? Wasn't he concerned that his universe wouldn't result in life, as was the case on Earth for many millions of simulated iterations?

He told her that his people had done a backward scan of time within their own universe to better understand it and its framework. Using advanced optics and some bending of the rules that would typically limit one's travel to the speed of light, they were able to see the beginning and determine how their universe took shape. They'd used that data to set the starting point for their new universe.

He told her that the process would slow upon the development of the advanced cellular structures that could evolve into sentient life. Until then, it would bull forward through simulated time its variables pre-selected for the formation of organic matter. The wall interface displayed a complex miasma of colors and shapes, a universe displayed in macro as it expeditiously built the nest that would house Grenn's offspring.

Dr. Sunder Davies, Simulation Department Head at Proxy

We were proud of the developments within Aurora, obviously. But there was still an unspoken...hesitancy about it. About how things had progressed.

I, for one, couldn't help but wonder if we'd wasted our time taking the technological paths we'd walked on Earth. Having been shown another means of universe-creation that seemed to be so much more effective and efficient, not to mention all the other developments the Aurorans seemed to take for granted, what good were we in comparison? What good was all the hard work we'd put in, generation after generation, when compared to this? What would happen if their tech was brought into our world? Would everything we'd accomplished be relegated to the annuls of history, replaced by this new collection of wonders?

I didn't have long to speculate. The activity on Grenn's wall was slowing noticeably, the once-frantic imagery settling into a normalized pace. The view scrolled in toward a galaxy, then a planet, and was soon focused on a landmass that looked like it could have been located on either Earth or Aurora. The land was green and brown, it was surrounded by blue water, and a slight distortion and cloudiness indicated it was surrounded by an atmosphere.

Grenn made another, different gesture, and the wall displayed an array of figures alongside the visual. Before we could get a good look at what the figures represented — numbers? letters? — a creature filled the screen.

The humanoid was a step further removed from Earth's humanity than Grenn and his people. If Aurorans were humans as explained through a game of telephone, this new creature was the result of two consecutive games.

They had the same three-and-three thumbs-to-digits arrangement on their hands, but their shoulders were pulled further back, slinging their arms out like wings. Their faces lacked noses like the Aurorans', but their eyes were very large, taking up a great deal of the 'empty' space found on the faces of Grenn's people. The legs on this new humanoid were reversed from those of humans, as was the case on the Aurorans, but they stood in a deeper crouch than Grenn's people, and had larger, flatter feet spread out very wide, allowing them to hold that stance. As a result they stood shorter than a human, but they looked to be as tall as an Auroran, if they were ever stretched out to their full vertical length.

Matthew Gruber, Chief Hardware Specialist at Proxy

Grenn nodded his head and touched the wall, and his image was projected into the universe, startling the group of the just-grown humanoids we'd been looking at.

Their eyes widened when Grenn lifted his palm to them. Grenn spoke to Pope as an aside, his projected image remaining still. "I've modified their mood by increasing their bodily excretion of calming chemicals. This also amplifies their awe and reduces their fear in the face of something new."

Pope clearly wanted to ask how he'd achieved this ability to control other humanoids, including those from a different species, but Grenn was already refocused on his creations, jabbering at them in a language that must have been their own. How it was he spoke this language, their species having just been created, we couldn't say for sure. I guessed it might be some kind of neural-scanning technology that isolated the areas of their brains that were stimulated when they spoke to each other, and then pulled images and sounds from that into auto-interpretation software.

Whatever it was, it seemed to work. The humanoids watched Grenn's projected image, nodded when he finished, and solemnly held their own palms up toward him as he raised his in farewell.

Maxine Richmond, Psychologist In Residence at Proxy

Having first met Grenn when he was an adolescent, it was fascinating to see him as a fully developed adult. To have the opportunity to study how an external force, in this case, people and ideas from another culture, could augment some aspects of a personality while tempering others.

Grenn was an ambitious young man when we first met him, but his ambitions manifested differently than they might have had he grown up Earth. On Aurora, his people pursued inner-development, and as such, their focus on meditation outweighed their desire to manipulate their environment with technology. They idealized making themselves fit happily into whatever space they found themselves occupying, while we on Earth are more likely to change our environments to suit us.

As a result, Grenn's ambition initially looked to us like a lack of ambition. He didn't build big, impressive things. He didn't lead other people. Instead, he looked inward and worked hard to be calm. At peace. He triggered our hook by activating more of his brain than anyone in his planet's history. Grenn did this through discipline and endurance. He focused on what he desired and made it manifest.

It was little surprise, then, when he told Dr. Pope that he'd interacted with the humanoids in the newly created universe so that he might provide them with values rather than just technology. He told them that theirs was a people destined for great things, but only if they were able to embrace the dual values of inward and outward growth. This was what had allowed Grenn and his people to flourish, and he wanted to share that prosperity with his people's children.

When Grenn spoke to his 'children,' he made them a promise. He would return, he said, in 200 years, and at that point he would create a doorway between their world and his. He said they were the caretakers of their universe, which was a responsibility and a gift.

He cleared the screen on the wall after saying farewell to the creatures within. The view shifted to show the crowd of his people back at the auditorium where Dr. Pope had been presented. He said to them, "Now let us see what our children," and then to Dr. Pope, "and your grandchildren," and then to everyone, "have accomplished."

Grenn gestured to clear the image on the wall, then once more to show an expanded view of a solar system. "They've reached other heavenly bodies," he said. "And in such a short time." He was stating fact, not bragging. The view zoomed in closer, passing small space stations and moon colonies. Satellites swarmed the periphery of the planet, though these were the only sign of movement above the clouds that covered much of the planet's surface. No other spacecraft were apparent.

The image cut through the clouds, stuttered, and stopped. Three of the planet's five major landmasses were…pockmarked. Cratered. A strange color, far more browns and grays than moments before during our first visit, 200 years previous in the new planet's timeline.

Grenn's lips tightened. It was the first visible sign of frustration I'd ever seen him express. He didn't stop, though. He zoomed in closer, moving his fingers as if gently wafting an aroma toward his face.

The remnants of vast cities were viewable from space. The ruins of smaller towns were scattered around the continents, the outlines of buildings could be seen as we got closer.

Grenn closed his eyes, paused, and said, "There is still life. Mostly non-sentient. But…" His eyes opened and the view flickered from where it was, hovering over one of the larger cities, to an expanse of wilderness. A trio of figures emerged from the underbrush. Their clothes were tattered, their humanoid faces a mess of abrasions and bruises, their enormous eyes wide. One of them was limping and barely staying upright on its elephantine feet. Another was helping the injured one lope forward. The third was…

"It's going to kill them," Dr. Pope said about the third humanoid, a cudgel of some sort in its hands, wielded like a baseball bat. It was a few dozen feet from swinging range.

Grenn watched as the creature ran toward the unarmed duo. The assailant had crossed half the distance when Grenn said, "No."

Time slowed inside the projection, and Grenn once again appeared within, standing between the attacker and its victims. Grenn said to them, "This is over. Come with me."

All three humanoids looked shocked, but there was a glimmer of recognition in their eyes. The creature with the weapon snarled and leapt forward in slow-motion, aiming the cudgel at Grenn's head. The two other humanoids cringed at the same sedate speed, bending their legs and pressing their bodies closer to the ground while extending their hands toward Grenn, palms up.

The screen went blank once more, and Grenn relaxed his body. He was once again fully there with Dr. Pope, on Aurora.

On the ground next to them, catching their breath and clinging to one another, were the two injured, pursued humanoids from the world on the wall.

FABRICATION

Joan Deacon, Chief Financial Officer at Proxy

I didn't want to be the one to say it. To remind everyone that we had a goldmine under our feet. Well, in our computers, on a lower universal rung. But it didn't seem like anyone else would.

Amelia returned to Earth from Aurora, and she insisted we allow Grenn some time with the two survivors he'd pulled up from his simulated universe. They agreed to meet up later and figure out what went wrong, and to sort out what the unfortunate events within Grenn's simulation meant for their endeavors to create life and other new universes.

Amelia slipped out of her virtual reality gear, went into her office, and closed the door. The rest of us just kind of looked at each other awkwardly, then went back to our own stations to process in the ways we each processed. Maybe get a little work done. Though my work was somewhat dependent on what happened next, so I waited and crossed my fingers that we'd still be good to get some of that glorious tech from Grenn's people. That way we could at least get the manufacturing and marketing gears turning. Begin the patent-filing rigamarole, at least.

I already had the cloud computer hardware chain in the works, though who we partnered with for construction, energy, and the like would depend on what else we learned from Grenn about manufacturing. We'd created a process for ourselves to use, which allowed us to print most of our own components and surreptitiously source the things we couldn't make in-house from hardware producers around the world. If anyone looked at just one portion of the supply chain they wouldn't know exactly what we were up to.

We'd planned to expand this and benefit from the cost-savings associated with scale, but based on what I'd seen done on Aurora, it seemed like we might want to slow down and wait for some of that action. Maybe we could leapfrog our own methods and start using and selling Grenn's, instead. It wouldn't make much sense to harden our supply chains and spin up for larger-scale production if we had the option of switching to something cheaper, cleaner, more powerful, and generally better in the near-future.

There was also the possibility we might find out that cloud computing technology was something we'd want to keep on the down-low for the moment. If it turned out that our core competency was farming high-tech civilizations, like Grenn's, for knowledge, then we wouldn't want to make it any easier for competitors to pop up, would we? I didn't want to see Dissipation or Crytical or Apple or some other tech company building their own universes, evolving their own simulated species, and bringing their own new inventions into markets we wanted to own.

Matthew Gruber, Chief Hardware Specialist at Proxy

Who gets to see something like that? Civilization-wide cataclysm.

Wow.

I don't mean to sound heartless about it, I really don't. Grenn was clearly distraught by the whole state of affairs, as well he should be. His purpose in helping us and developing the technological backbone of his world, not to mention laboring for a few hundred years until we finally reappeared, was to create life. To ensure that the life he created would be happy. To spread goodness, not just in his own universe, but in all universes. The kid was a goddamn saint.

But he failed. It certainly wasn't his fault, because who could know what other variables were at play? Who could know what impact his words or actions had on the timeline of the universe his people created? It's possible things would have gone sideways even if he hadn't made contact, or maybe turned out even worse. Maybe he spared them all a lot of pain by ensuring that the bad things happened quickly. Maybe in saving those two humanoids from the dying world, he did the best anyone could have done under the circumstances.

It definitely complicated things, whatever the case. Grenn was our connection to a world that created and wielded technologies that had to be at least a hundred years ahead of our own in sophistication. He also came from a society that'd managed to intertwine technology with ethics in a way we'd yet to achieve anywhere on Earth. Grenn had a whole lot to offer, so long as we could keep him on the right track. So long as we could keep him focused on goals that ran parallel to our own.

Unfortunately, there were a lot things that could upset that balance. He could decide that technology was to blame for his sub-universe's destruction and start some kind of anti-tech revolution. He could have a philosophical epiphany that would lead to cutting ties with other universes completely, including ours. He might ban the creation of life in general, which would mean no more universes created within his universe. Or he could have a counter-pacifist kick, causing his weaponless society to quickly arm itself and faction up the way scared groups of otherwise well-meaning people have throughout Earth's history.

Maybe Grenn would simply allow the moment to pass and throw himself into other pursuits. To a maybe-immortal, very wise person, that might seem to be the most logical response.

These concerns were extra relevant to me. I wanted to learn how immortality was achieved. I wanted to know how they powered their civilization, and how they managed to integrate controlled mutation and tech into their personal biomes. I wanted to visit other solar systems.

I wanted a frickin' spaceship.

Though I could only see their world through a graphical interface, I wanted to be there. And although that wasn't possible, there wasn't any reason we couldn't bring what they had to Earth. To our universe.

No reason except, possibly, the fractured emotions of a person we'd created and then entrusted with everything.

Stephanie Baxter, Biologist In Residence at Proxy

It was heartbreaking. The look on Grenn's face.

It wasn't that he outwardly emoted. His people had mostly weaned themselves off of such responses, expressing themselves in other ways. But after watching him for so long and knowing how to read his vitals, it was clear that he was having the worst day of his life. And understandably so.

I honestly wasn't sure how to feel after we saw what we saw. It was a tragedy, of course, because there was a whole planet of human-like people destroyed in some kind of war. Only a few left. And of those survivors, one was trying to kill the other two. It didn't say very nice things about society.

The placating response was that those weren't humans. They were derived from the human model insomuch as Grenn's people evolved in very similar circumstances as we did, and these new creatures an off-shoot of that. They were humanoids. Bipeds. Circulatory system. Carbon-based. Large, complex brains. We evolved life that we could relate to and got the Aurorans. Grenn did the same, and got…a few survivors.

Our feelings on the matter were merely academic, though. What would happen next was Grenn's decision, not ours. We could still create other universes. We could then nest deeper universes inside of those. Even if the experiment with Grenn and his people and Aurora was a failure in the business sense, we would be fine. We could still learn a lot from Grenn's people and perhaps bring some of their technologies into our universe, even if they did not wish to continue universe-building on Aurora.

All we could do in the meantime was wait to see which way Grenn's attitude swayed. We could watch and hope.

Dr. Sunder Davies, Simulation Department Head at Proxy

It was tempting to wonder if we were making a big deal out of nothing. If we were caught up in our own simulation. Because what was our simulated universe except an incredibly complex video game? What was a failure within such a game other than a plot twist, a hurdle to be leaped? A problem within a fake place, created for our pleasure and benefit, for our entertainment?

It was tempting to see Aurora and Grenn and all of his people as surprising and challenging, but also something we could wrangle. Something that seemed out of our control, but which was ultimately fully within our jurisdiction.

What were simulated lives, after all, other than ones and zeroes in complex arrangements? What were the particles that made up Grenn's universe other than measurements taken from our own, and then replicated using numbers inside of sandbox software? What was the drama of Grenn's efforts in universe-creation except a compelling sub-storyline within the storyline we'd created? Wasn't it just an evolution of something we'd set in motion at the beginning? The numerically predictable outcome that, had we the math for it, we could have prepared for? Seen coming?

Of course, none of that was true. It wasn't true because we had developed randomness, and the same process run again from the same starting point would yield different results. And if Grenn and his people were just numbers, well, so were we. Perhaps our particles were manifested in different ways, within different ether, but our reality was still based on math. Still based on what amounted to ones and zeroes inside God's computer.

Maxine Richmond, Psychologist In Residence at Proxy

It was a quiet, thoughtful, anticipatory day. So much had happened in such a short period that, despite the incredible success of the technologies they had built, and the world they had birthed, the team was struggling with the unforeseen consequences of their actions.

Seeing how Grenn had grown in the two Auroran centuries since we'd last seen him created months of work for me. The amount of data we had collected was immense, and though I had some idea of what was going on in Grenn's head, and perhaps even what he might do next, there were still many variables I needed to interpret and incorporate. There were myriad potential deviances from thought-patterns and response-structures I'd worked out for the younger version of Grenn that I needed to rework.

As with many aspects of the project, though, my hopes and expectations didn't neatly align with what actually happened.

The day after Dr. Pope's dramatic reintroduction to Grenn and the Auroran people, I arrived at the office to find that our fabricator had worked through the night and had produced two new human-shaped figures. These simulacra were of a different make than the one we'd created for Grenn, his so-called robatar. Aesthetically simpler, somewhat streamlined. They made greater use of ceramic and polymers, while ours had more visible metal components.

Matthew Gruber, Chief Hardware Specialist at Proxy

Maxine was already there when I walked into the machine shop, and was talking to Grenn, who was wearing his robatar body. There were two other figures there, too, standing a little out of the way, but listening in on the conversation between the shrink and the immortal boy from another universe.

The fabricator was still operating, producing some complex-looking ceramic machine components with integrated processors that I couldn't identify for certain; energy storage cells, maybe.

I was greeted as I entered the machine shop, first by Grenn, and then by each of his guests: one named Reyko, and the other named Tryko. It took me a moment to realize that these weren't fellow Aurorans, they were the duo that survived the destruction of their world, two universes below our own.

Knowing this, their simulacra made more sense. The arms were slung further back, pushing their elbows far out to the side, and their legs were reversed, their feet huge. These were designs modeled on their actual biologies. I wondered if Grenn was wildly uncomfortable seeing our world through lenses attached to a humanesque body, rather than one more closely resembling his own Auroran anatomy.

It was weird, having the three of them just there, in the office, waiting for us. But the awesome kind of weird. I mean, it's strange enough to be talking to artificial life in a robotic avatar, right? But even more so when there are three of them, and two of the three are models that you didn't design. Something that no one from your planet, your universe, designed.

As I tried to peek past him and get a better look at what was being fabricated, Grenn apologized for his behavior the day before. He seemed to think he had been a complete jerk to the team, though anyone without the instrumentation to measure his most minute physiological readings wouldn't have perceived any difference in his words or mannerism.

Grenn explained that he'd meditated on the issue since we last saw him the day before, which was one Earth day and one Auroran day, since we were at the moment synced up, time-wise. He said that he'd come to three conclusions.

The first was that he had been too limited in his thinking. It was his ambition to create life, and in doing so to increase the amount of happy, fulfilled consciousnesses in existence. This was a flawed approach, he decided, because although it did have the intended end-benefit, it back-burnered the life that already existed throughout his universe, and ours. He had an open dialogue and strong connection with a species, us humans, who already had many of the technologies required to convey much of what he wanted to share, and his plans weren't taking advantage of this. It was hubris on his part, he said, and he was sorry.

I should note that he was kind enough not to apply this same standard to, ahem, a certain other species who had created lower-level universes for far less moral reasons.

The second conclusion was that we needed better designations for the universes we were interacting with, as it would save us a lot of time to have a common language around such things. Grenn suggested we use the identifier 'Universe 0' or 'U0' for short, for our universe which contained Earth, which would mark it as the core universe in the stack. His universe, which contained Aurora, would be Universe -1 or U-1, which would indicate that it's one level below U0 in the universal stack. The universe that Reyko and Tryko were pulled from, then, would be U-2.

Grenn's third conclusion, and one that he hesitated before presenting, perhaps because he thought it would be difficult for us to hear, was proposed as a question. He said, "If your universe is U0, and my universe is U-1…how might we establish contact with U+1?"

Dr. Sunder Davies, Simulation Department Head at Proxy

This was a concept many of us had considered, of course. Only individually, though. It hadn't come up at work.

It had probably been mulled over for generations by people who used different terminology than we were using, actually. We wondered if our reality might be just a simulation in another reality's laboratory, people from the late 20th century wondered if reality was a hologram, those from the Renaissance period wondered if reality was an illusion, and so on.

The concept of 'heaven' and other versions of an afterlife so pervaded faiths from around the world that I couldn't help but wonder if there might be some kind of collective memory embedded in humankind's DNA. A remembrance of moments from throughout our ancestral history during which the universal ceiling had been breached, or maybe even operated in a different way. Tales which reference visitors from a higher plane, another world. Like Pope in her avatar had been in Grenn's world. A god among men.

But it was all just speculation, and we were focusing on

concrete science and how to apply it as technology. Anything beyond that, even if it was tangentially related and potentially very interesting, seemed like a distraction and inappropriate for the workplace.

Until Grenn brought it up.

Joan Deacon, Chief Financial Officer at Proxy

The revelation that Grenn wanted to go further up than our universe was super exciting.

Not just because it would be interesting and maybe explain some fundamental things about reality and whatever. It also meant that we'd have to reverse the flow of technology and prioritize bringing tech from his world into ours, just as we'd done with Earth tech introduced to Aurora several centuries back.

And that meant bringing all kinds of stuff to Earth for me to assess and brand and market. It meant building a new infrastructure with income-positive revenue streams, which would be a complete one-eighty from where we'd been for so long, pretty much just hemorrhaging cash financial quarter after financial quarter.

And! We'd get to do to our world what Grenn had done to his. We'd be bringing these futuristic technologies to a culture that didn't even know they were coming. It would be the biggest challenge ever, and I couldn't wait to see what we had to work with. Even the simplest of innovations could be game-changers, and could establish us as the dominant player in a bunch of different fields.

We would have to structure things in such a way that the public didn't start to question how we were doing what we were doing as such a small company. We'd have to create product cycles that seemed believable, even if they were remarkable. We'd have to fill the planet with awesome stuff and make it seem normal.

Stephanie Baxter, Biologist In Residence at Proxy

Joan was aflutter like I'd never seen her before. She was thrilled to finally bring more of her skills to bear. But we were all pretty jazzed.

There was a slight shadow cast over the imminent adventure, though. There was still the unanswered question of how seeding a civilization with knowledge and technologies from beyond their evolutionary scope impacted them and their offspring.

We gave Grenn and his people information and know-how that was far beyond what they had developed themselves. The result was positive for them, but negative for the people in their sub-universe, U-2. Grenn's simulated offspring pulled themselves apart. Brutally.

I don't think any of us believed there was a one-to-one correlation between spreading knowledge and destroying worlds, but could there be an associative one? And if so, how strong would it be? A one percent increase in the chances of self-destruction? Ten percent? Ninety-nine percent? And what level of risk would be acceptable? At what point do the benefits of increased knowledge disappear under the weight of an increasingly likely apocalypse?

Maxine Richmond, Psychologist In Residence at Proxy

There was an unspoken but very real toll on the team as a result of what happened in U-2. No one assigned blame for the cataclysm, or even necessarily worried that it would happen again. The reality of a civilization-wide cataclysm, however, was itself so horrible that no one seemed to have taken the time to fully comprehend it. When a snippet of memory of the desolation, or a wisp of a U-2 related thought crossed someone's mind, you could see it written all over their face.

This was most pronounced when work was done collaboratively with Reyko and Tryko. The pair had proven themselves to be marvelous technologists, as most individuals on their world had been, apparently. Interacting so intimately with the survivors of such an event, however, survivors who had seen the buildup, the war, and the annihilation of their species, brought troubled thoughts to the surface more frequently.

Schematics and research were transmitted from U-1 through the hook software, which had been augmented by Grenn's people to allow for a higher bandwidth. On Earth, U0 in the new universe-focused vernacular, Mr. Gruber and Dr. Davies processed the data as it arrived, and explained to Ms. Deacon what it offered in terms of technology and overall scientific development for Earth. She then worked this information into her business roadmap which outlined when each component should be unleashed on the public, and how best to present it.

Reyko and Tryko spent a great deal of their time at the Proxy lab, helping to explain the more complex concepts so that we Earthlings could understand them. The pair were also more than competent in determining how the manufacturing of some materials and technologies might be accomplished on a planet that didn't yet have the proper infrastructure in place.

Despite their helpfulness and willingness to put in long hours of work, a wake of grimaces and misty eyes followed the duo from U-2. Even viewing the Proxy team's responses through robotic lenses, I can't imagine Reyko and Tryko were ignorant as to how those around them were responding to their presence.

Eugene Crisp, Chief Storyteller at Proxy

The effort to bring U-1 technologies to Earth was underway shortly after the arrival of the U-2 survivors. The mechanical avatars in which Reyko, Tryko, and Grenn lived while on Earth were some of the first pieces of hardware to be upgraded.

But before those upgrades came the new fabricators. Three iterations of fabricators were required to produce some of the machines we'd need to funnel data from U-1 to Earth, and to make use of those schematics. As such, after producing simple simulacra for Reyko and Tryko to inhabit, Grenn began fabricating the components of an upgraded fabricator, which was capable of 'printing' machine parts at a higher resolution, and using different materials than our own. That new fabricator was then used to produce another fabricator, which was too advanced to produce with our previous model, but was within the capabilities of the new one Grenn had printed. That second fabricator printed a third, and that tertiary iteration was the version we'd be using for a while. It was capable of printing exotic materials, working with matter directly and recompiling it into whatever it required for a given task, and even working with energy in a way we Earthlings had trouble understanding, but which was a core principle that allowed the Aurorans to transfer energy, information, and even matter instantly across their global grid. This was the technology that allowed them to teleport with such ease, while also ensuring that the energy storage and production nodes didn't 'leak' heat or radiation.

Diagrams were transmitted through the hook, and were loaded into the fabricators to produce the machine infrastructure we we lacking. Digital interfaces which allowed us humans to more easily tap into and explore the knowledge base Grenn's people shared were also downloaded.

The Auroran 'grid,' through which they shuttled energy and matter around, was similar in many ways to Earth's internet, but was far more integrated into their society. Their grid controlled the flow of energy, matter, and information between nodes, and those nodes consisted of fabricators, individuals, and energy production resources. Energy was generated through reclamation devices that captured most of the energy expended by their people, including the vibrations of footsteps and the energy used by their internal organs. They made use of some of the same energy sources we used on earth, such as solar cells, hydro- and air-turbines, and geothermal gatherers, and they also channeled a type of energy that Grenn had trouble describing accurately, but which involved harnessing gravity in a way that we were far from even attempting on Earth. That, and many other things that were far beyond our present understanding and capabilities, would come later.

Through the hook-based interface to which we had been given access, we could also interact with every individual on Aurora through their grid, as every single member of their species was a node on their network. I once asked Grenn why they decided to connect to each other through one, massive, centralized network, and what ramifications this might have for their culture. What happens to privacy under such conditions? Wouldn't some kind of external interface, like a removable, perhaps wearable device, be preferable? To allow the flexibility of communal connection alongside the option to disconnect from a potentially overwhelming amount of information and interaction?

Grenn told me that in their culture, interaction with the community and access to information were interwoven with the individual in a different way than on Earth. While we humans connected with each other out of practicality, to share information and disseminate culture, Aurorans did it to fill themselves with each other's being. They were, in a sense, individual components of something larger, and biotech had allowed them to augment their brains in so that the existing connection they already felt was amplified.

I asked him where it would stop, if it would stop, and whether he thought the people of Earth had the same potential for connectivity. To this he said that of course we were capable, but taking such a path may not be ideal for us. As to where it stopped, he told me that he didn't yet know. He and his people were still walking their own path, and they couldn't see the end of it, if indeed an end existed.

His guess was that there was no end.

Matthew Gruber, Chief Hardware Specialist at Proxy

About six months after we began parsing the information and specs we'd received from U-1, we were in a pretty good spot.

Grenn, Reyko, and Tryko were with us in the lab most of the time, inhabiting a trio of incredibly realistic simulacra. It was hard to call them robots or even robatars at that point, because some of the components were lab-grown organic materials, interwoven with the fiber-optics, spun-metal, and other artificial ingredients. Each of their individual simulacrum looked and moved like their respective species, as well, so Grenn looked like an Auroran, and Reyko and Tryko looked like denizens of U-2. They were there to greet us each morning, interacting with the team as if they'd been working in the Proxy lab since the very beginning.

The three visitors still didn't get a lot of our humor, or what passed for humor in such a geeky setting, but they'd learned to laugh when we did, and gave appreciative nods when they weren't sure if something was funny or not. They worked overnight after the rest of us had gone home, since they didn't need sleep the way we did. One of the benefits of existing virtually in a fabricated body in another universe, I guess.

After a few months, I could barely remember what things were like before we had such incredibly knowledgeable alien colleagues around to ask for help and to learn from. To brainstorm new ideas with.

That was one of the more remarkable things about our guests, actually. Despite the fact that they were far ahead of us in so many ways, they never ceased to be curious and open to new ideas, approaches, and outside input. Which helped when any of us humans would wonder about our own insignificance in the three-world system we'd set up. Sure, we'd started the whole thing, but it was easy to get derailed and spiral down a fiction in which we were replaced or outmoded or, perhaps worst of all, ignored as worthless by our very creations. Bypassed and left out of the adventure.

It was the science lab equivalent of a child surpassing their parents, I guess. Leaving home, never calling or visiting because of how irrelevant their parents had become to their child's life. We were worried about that possibility.

Our three visitors made sure we never felt that way, though, which is a big part of why the tricornered relationship worked so well.

Stephanie Baxter, Biologist In Residence at Proxy

There were moments during those six months of learning and building in which we had to make some pretty significant decisions.

When our exploration of the U-1 grid showed us their genetic manipulation processes and findings, we were suddenly one step away from being able to augment humans the way Grenn and his people were augmented. Of being able to connect ourselves to one another, biologically. Or connect ourselves to a larger network like they had on Aurora. We could even 'upgrade' our capabilities in a way that would grant us access to larger portions of our brains, providing the ability to remember things with greater clarity and predictability. We could adjust a gene that would help auto-cleanse garbage neural cells so that we wouldn't need to sleep, or at least not sleep as often. We could extend and regenerate telomeres so that aging would slow and eventually cease.

Matthew and I argued over what should be done with this information, as the rest of the team stood by and watched. I was of the opinion that we should proceed slowly. We didn't know how the differences between Grenn's humanoid species and ours would impact the results of their studies. We didn't know what changes would occur should we proceed with their processes without making our own, human-focused changes. Matthew thought that the genetic differences would be minuscule enough that any deviations from their findings would be correctable.

Grenn, Reyko, and Tryko gave zero input, as was their policy when such questions arose. They didn't want to influence the outcome of our discussions at all.

Dr. Pope stepped in and said that we would focus on puncturing up to U+1 before experimenting with, or releasing to the public, the genetic augmentation findings. Then we would move full-throttle to bring such discoveries to market and make them as widely available as possible. "One massive societal shift at a time," she said.

She was right. We had to seed society with some of the less-advanced technologies we'd been handed first, and that would be a full-time job. The revelation that we'd created sub-universes, and that we were potentially within some other universe's sub-universe, and that this universe stack might go on infinitely, would blow minds. The last thing we needed while having that discussion, as a species, was the simultaneous introduction of genome-altering technologies from the future. Technologies that would allow the human race to permanently change itself, carve out new social dynamics, and upheave the modern world as we knew it.

Matthew Gruber, Chief Hardware Specialist at Proxy

I was upset, yes. And I still maintain that augmenting our brains to make ourselves smarter and more capable, not to mention removing the necessity for sleep, would have allowed us to reach our goals faster.

But I get why Pope decided what she did. I didn't like it, but I understood it.

So, because becoming superhuman wasn't on the menu just yet, I spent my attention on how we might puncture up. How we might find a hook dropped down into our universe by a theoretical species that may have created us within a simulation they'd built in their universe, just as we'd created U-1 and Aurora.

The most obvious first step was to explore the paths already tread by other researchers at that point in time. The EAGLE Project, for example, had created universe simulations from observations of the Cosmic Microwave Background. This eventually led them to look further, searching those ancient photons for some indication of how our universe was created.

Other researchers tried to push the boundaries of exploration, assuming that technologies running a universe-wide simulation would necessarily simplify that universe, as we had with Aurora and the universe in which it existed. This theoretical simulation would only fully resolve observed aspects of the universe it contained. The mitochondrial world, then, would only be rendered in detail after we'd discovered it, as would the macro expanse of interstellar space. These researchers thought that by looking further both outward and inward, we may be able to force the computer simulating our universe to stutter in a way that we could measure.

Setting aside the obvious, potentially cataclysmic downsides of making the system that simulates our universe stutter, it seemed to me that there had to be a better way.

Based on our simulations and the system we built to create it, I couldn't fathom a scenario in which the creators of a simulated universe would be so limited by software and hardware that the denizens of their faux-world would be able to glitch the system. We didn't have any trouble with the capabilities of our cloud systems, despite the massive technological developments in Grenn's universe. Because we had based their reality on concepts and then adjusted those concepts *in situ* based on other stimuli, which were also rendered as concepts, our processors weren't at all strained. We defined the idea of an 'atom' so that every atom in Grenn's world was merely referencing that definition, rather than building each and every atom from scratch, which would have used a lot more processing power. It took a decent amount of processing power to render these concepts initially, but very little to reference them from that point forward.

This is what would allow for a surplus processing power as we went even deeper into lower level simulations, and it's what kept those of us who'd built simulations from running out of capacity.

In short, a species capable of simulating a universe is capable of keeping it from glitching. Any error visible from the inside would have to be intentional, which is why I believed that our best bet was finding a hook dropped into our universe by that higher-stack species. Something intentional, something they meant for us to find.

So what would such a hook look like? How would we go about finding it? And how might we reach out and grab it, once it was found?

WHERE

Eugene Crisp, Chief Storyteller at Proxy

After those first six months of having access to U-1's grid, Dr. Pope gave Ms. Deacon the green light to roll out the next phase of the plan: unfurling the pre-planned business infrastructure beyond the Proxy lab.

This step consisted of several mini-steps, the first of which was the import of U-1 technologies into U0, which meant bringing Aurora's intellectual riches to the whole of Earth, rather than keeping it relegated to Proxy's office.

Umbrella corporations were founded to hold the intellectual property until such a time that it could be safely released into a public trust for the thronging billions. We determined that simply dumping the data onto the internet or making it accessible for corporations or governments to paw over would be the wrong move, the former because it would put significant power in the hands of too many before ethics and societal norms existed to contain them, and the latter because established structures would suddenly wield even more power than they already did, incentivizing them to reinforce their own borders and bank accounts at the expense of others. A land-grab would ensue, and those with the ability to lock down information and control industrial channels would do so. There would be more autocracy, war, and, quite possibly, the self-implosion of humanity before it had a chance to make full use of these new, wonderful gifts.

This in mind, a more iterative, inclusive, restrained process was called for.

Ms. Deacon took the lead on this, bringing in outside business and legal consultants with expertise in fields ranging from telecommunications to food distribution, from clean energy to polymers, from genetic engineering to governmental theory. She kept them close enough that she could feed them theoreticals and gain their insights, but far enough that none of them would ever suspect they were involved with something like what Proxy had.

Proxy, Inc. became the silent backer of these umbrella companies, which in turn sprouted smaller holding companies that filed patents, invested in infrastructure like real estate and machinery, and began building a network of relationships. Joan managed this expansive enterprise and seemed happier than any of us had ever seen her, despite the sheer number of balls she was juggling and the potential for extreme consequences should any of them hit the ground.

Maxine Richmond, Psychologist In Residence at Proxy

The Aurorans had developed a 'grid' which allowed them to send and receive energy and matter similarly to how we send information through the internet. I was told the analogy wasn't a perfect one, but the specifics of the technology weren't as important as what it meant for society.

Within U-1, transportation was achieved by scanning a person's exact physical state, including their brain chemistry. The data from that scan was then transmitted to another place on the grid, where they were recompiled from raw matter, from the quantum level upward.

The troubling aspect of this technology was that the original, pre-teleportation body and mind were destroyed in the process; pulled apart and added to the general supply of matter. That matter would be recompiled as a fully functioning, living person elsewhere, but from different matter. The person was the same, because the scan of them at the moment of transport was used to rebuild them on the other side. But they were different in a sense, as well.

Scientifically, the difference in a person's biology before and after traveling this way was unmeasurable. But socially? Such a means of transportation worked for the Aurorans because they had long been comfortable with death, and had culturally evolved to not view it as the loss of a life, but rather the return of their energy to a greater whole. They were also comfortable with the idea of being part of a community, even at the subatomic level, whereas humans more have typically celebrated their individuality.

Would humanity be comfortable with technologies which

allowed for the unlimited and instantaneous transfer of matter if they had to die and be reborn as a clone of themselves in the tradeoff? What other mental gymnastics would be required for our species to benefit from these futuristic gifts?

Joan Deacon, Chief Financial Officer at Proxy

Finally able to flex my massive biz-muscles, I had a blast setting up cloaked accounts and umbrella corporations, making sure there were mountains of paperwork and piles of unmemorable logos between Proxy and the technologies we were patenting.

It was only a couple of months before I negotiated our first sale of a device schematic. In Aurora's grid, we found an older bit of tech that created an instantaneous, untraceable link between two devices. A link that somehow involved quantum physics, and which allowed for the development of a new generation of personal devices that were untappable and untraceable by anyone outside of the intended recipient. No government, hacker, or anyone else could listen in on these connections. Valuable!

This was a stepping stone technology for Grenn's people, and was eventually incorporated into their grid, built in to everyone's genetic makeup. For our purposes, though, the handheld device version was perfect. There were companies, individuals, and governments who would pay immense amounts of money to ensure their conversations weren't being listened in on.

It also fit squarely within the believability spectrum. These communicators weren't so advanced that people would ask questions about where we got the tech, or how we could afford the R&D. It made use of technologies we already understood, like quantum entanglement and communications hardware, but in a new, clever way.

I negotiated a one-year exclusivity agreement with a major technology company, one that had excellent distribution channels internationally, and which sold to governments, businesses, and consumers. After that, we'd make the patent licensable by anyone who wanted it, and would leak an open source version of the early device schematics to the internet, if a good one hadn't already become available in the meantime.

This seemed to be the ideal way to get this specific technology, and all the U-1 tech we eventually wanted to see spread far and wide on Earth, to the masses. There would no doubt be tweaks needed, but it was a step worth celebrating.

Amelia threw us a big party at a nearby bowling alley to celebrate the occasion. We all drank skillfully and bowled badly and had a marvelous time. We shambled into the office the next day, a little hungover but excited to keep moving forward, now that our efforts were on the verge of changing the world. Hopefully for the better.

Matthew Gruber, Chief Hardware Specialist at Proxy

It was a really clever means of distribution. The scheme was elegant, and it allowed us to plant seeds, rather than trying to install full-grown trees everywhere. Metaphorical alien trees that people might not like, or that might kill everyone who came into contact with them.

We wanted people to see and feel the evolution of this tech, rather than waking up one day to find their world had been turned upside-down. We wanted these concepts shown at technology conferences and talked about on social networks. We wanted them to come about in a natural-seeming way, at a natural-seeming pace. To do otherwise would scare a lot of people, or at least disenfranchise them.

The time for wondering would come eventually, and we hoped to be able to sit down and talk about everything openly at that point. Proxy's initial innovation, Aurora, U-2, everything. But we had to keep it all on the down low for a time, and not cast any suspicion. Otherwise we might invite unwelcome attention from antagonistic outside players with less benevolent goals.

Maxine Richmond, Psychologist In Residence at Proxy

On the morning after the bowling alley party, Grenn greeted us as we walked into the office, as usual. Unusual was that there was only one other simulacrum with him rather than two.

Mr. Gruber was telling a story about one of Dr. Davies' more entertaining bowling throws the night before, when Dr. Pope interrupted to ask why Reyko was absent.

Grenn said, quite matter-of-factly, that Reyko had deleted himself the night before, while we were away at the bowling alley. "He didn't wish to alarm anyone," Grenn told us, when asked what he meant. "But he didn't feel that his continued existence would be of further value. He decided the alternative was a more favorable option."

Dr. Baxter asked what he meant. What alternative?

Grenn replied, "Reyko has returned his energy to the universe."

Eugene Crisp, Chief Storyteller at Proxy

It was as if the air had been sucked out of the room.

The team went silent, several mouths hung open in surprise, in shock, while other faces went blank, their reflex to shut down and retreat rather than display the repulsion or sadness or fear or confusion they were feeling.

After a few silent moments, Dr. Pope asked Grenn why Reyko had decided on that course of action.

Grenn told her that the events of his world ending had been too much for Reyko. The things he'd had to do to survive, the things done to him by others, a lifetime of tortures endured. Even for a strong, self-aware consciousness, it was too much. He wished, instead, to return his energy to the whole, in the hope that it might one day be a part of a being who experienced a more favorable existence.

Dr. Baxter filled the silence that followed by asking how a digital entity ends its life.

Grenn explained that it was a matter of willing it to be so. To give up sustaining one's existence. To scramble the orderly math that manifested consciousness within a digital medium. While he spoke, Dr. Pope retreated to her office, closing the door behind her and pulling the blinds.

It was an unusual response from someone who was typically in control, and the team seemed to decide unanimously, but without saying a word, that they would neither comment upon nor question her actions. Instead, they told a few stories about Reyko, what few they had, since the visitor had only been a part of their team for a matter of months, and offered a cheers to his memory with their coffee mugs before one by one shuffling away to their respective corners of the office and laboratory.

Dr. Sunder Davies, Simulation Department Head at Proxy

Work from that moment was more routine and less celebratory. We were still excited about what we were doing, and about our goal to puncture up to U+1, but the road seemed to lead toward an indistinct horizon. That goal had once seemed very close, but Reyko's death, his digital suicide, seemed to slow our momentum a little.

Fortunately, the work that had to be done was also primarily iterative rather than groundbreaking. We were distributing technologies to help build an infrastructure that would allow us to detect a hook that may have been built by a theoretical species one level above us, while at the same time girding Earthly society in preparation for the other universe-related revelations we had in the pipeline.

Finding the theoretical hook would take years if we were lucky, decades if we weren't, and even then there would be no guarantee of success. We didn't even know if a hook existed, much less if there was a universe above us to begin with.

The time between would be filled with smaller victories as we increased the quality of life and level of happiness for humankind to the best of our collective ability. Grenn's philosophy proved a port in the storm for us in this regard, as it allowed us to focus on fulfilling a utilitarian goal while still moving steadily toward a discovery that was large and fundamental.

Matthew Gruber, Chief Hardware Specialist at Proxy

We decided during this period to make lot of the straight-up scientific knowledge we'd acquired from the Auroran grid available to humanity by divvying it out to universities, think-tanks, and other established players in the general knowledge industry.

We didn't make a dime on any of these efforts, and in fact spent quite a bit of the capital coming in from Joan's patent licensing efforts to fund certain studies and to surreptitiously point the scientists conducting them in the right direction. If we knew a particular material was possible, for instance, we could fund research that was looking for such a material, or which included work that might discover that material as a byproduct. It was a means of getting valuable information into textbooks without it seeming like that knowledge came from scientists in another universe.

Eugene Crisp, Chief Storyteller at Proxy

For the next year, the work days were long, the roadblocks were often difficult, but the rewards were enough that the momentum never abated. The Proxy staff could finally see the consequences of their efforts out in the real world, beyond the confines of their lab and office and machine shop, and that provided fuel to push through moments of doubt or difficulty.

It was a time of road paving, not battle. It was a time of reinforcement, not realignment. For much of the team it felt as if, for the first time, this adventure they'd joined might actually be sustainable. Rather than proving to be fireworks, exploding in a fiery burst of impressive and short-lived physics, their efforts might be an ever-growing eternal flame, first maintained by human hands, then upgraded to electric light, followed thereafter by technologies that remove the necessity for human maintenance entirely. A project that could outlive them all.

While engaged in these duties, this expansion of their research, this slow percolation of technologies into welcoming markets, the reinvigoration of their own social lives outside of their Proxy family, they sometimes spared a moment to wonder what was taking place behind Dr. Pope's office door. They wondered, not often but sometimes, what efforts their leader might be undertaking that she was unwilling or unable to share just yet. What it might mean for their own work. How it might upset the balance they'd established while removed from her Caesaresque influence.

Dr. Pope hadn't entirely disappeared from the team's radar. She would exchange a few words in passing and would ask about elements of their work that she'd read about in the company's activity log. After the details were explained, though, she would typically grunt and nod her head, retreating back into her own thoughts, seemingly distracted by something else. Something that was, much like Dr. Pope herself, adjacent to but separate from the work the rest of the team was doing.

The buildup to Dr. Pope's revelation isn't well-documented. It's known from her online searches and book purchases that, after Reyko's suicide, she began researching a field of study called 'thanatology,' which is the scientific study of death. It's also known that during this period she began to reach out to a new community, one that was very different from her usual associations.

Stephanie Baxter, Biologist In Residence at Proxy

We didn't have a typical office set up because we weren't a typical office. So when the buzzer went off, indicating that someone was at the front door, I was startled.

I was in the kitchen eating lunch, so I checked the door. There was a woman there. A very striking woman. She said she had a meeting with Dr. Pope, and that her name was Victoria Rose. I asked her to wait a second and I knocked at Dr. Pope's door. She said through the door, "Has Ms. Rose arrived?" I told her yes. She said let the woman in, bring her on back.

Ms. Rose sauntered in, hips pivoting. She gave me a wink before entering Dr. Pope's office. Obviously I did an online search of her name, and she dominated the first page of search results. So to speak.

She was a dominatrix.

Michael Hutchins, janitor at Proxy

I figured it was none of my business what the woman did in her spare time. Free country, isn't it? And Dr. Pope, she worked hard.

I didn't see what all the fuss was about. Modern world, modern lady. We've all tried things. Whatever was goin' on, good for her for gettin' hers, I say.

Eugene Crisp, Chief Storyteller at Proxy

Rumors of the salacious variety were few and far between at the Proxy offices. Not only were they misaligned with the professional respect each team member had for the other, but the opportunity for interpersonal scandal seldom emerged. Ms. Deacon was the most socially active person in the office, and even she had little in terms of a life outside of Proxy.

But a casual mention of the word 'dominatrix' or 'fetish' or anything sexual, particularly in regard to Dr. Pope, was enough to raise eyebrows. The personal aspect of our leader's life wasn't concealed so much as irrelevant. Dr. Pope was larger than life, professionally and intellectually, so questions like 'Is she seeing anyone?' never entered anyone's mind. It wasn't even clear what type of person, or gender, she might be interested in, if, indeed, she was interested in anyone romantically.

This dominatrix revelation, then, pulled many unknowns into the sunlight, and spurred some whispered conversations.

Ms. Victoria Rose visited the Proxy offices twice more after her initial visit. On her second visit, she arrived with a two-man crew who hauled large black boxes of the kind you might see at music venues, containing the band's sound equipment. The boxes were brought into Dr. Pope's office and then the men left, leaving Ms. Rose and Dr. Pope together for three hours. The men came back afterward, hauled the boxes back out, and Ms. Rose left with them.

On the third and final visit, the men brought their boxes once more, and Ms. Rose stayed with Dr. Pope in her office for over five hours, beginning in the early afternoon. This overlapped with the end of the work day, and much of the staff looked at Dr. Pope's door and exchanged meaningful, curious glances as they left the building, headed for the parking lot.

Dr. Baxter lingered. She needed a sign-off from Dr. Pope on an equipment requisition for the lab, an accessory for one of the fabricators that would allow her to print biological matter. It was an important component that she needed posthaste, and wasn't something she could easily fabricate in-lab.

She waited for over an hour, hoping that Dr. Pope's 'meeting' would end and she would be able to get the signature without interrupting. After that hour, she decided that, not having heard anything salacious through the relatively thin walls, it was probably safe to knock. If there was anything untoward going on inside, they'd let her know. Would tell her to wait.

Stephanie Baxter, Biologist In Residence at Proxy

I knocked on the door and didn't get a response. I knocked a little louder. Still nothing.

I turned the door knob slightly. It gave. It wasn't locked.

I cracked the door and just peeked in. I said through the opening, "Dr. Pope, I just need your signature on something before I leave."

But through the crack I saw something horrible.

Dr. Pope was strapped into some kind of device. Her face was blueish purple. Her neck was clearly constricted, and blood flow was blocked.

I pushed the door open and stumbled toward her, but was grabbed by Ms. Rose who was sitting off to one side. She said, "No, wait."

I was freaking out. Was this woman killing Dr. Pope? Was it some kind of sex thing? Might it have gone wrong? Dr. Pope looked dead. It must have gone wrong. I pulled away from Ms. Rose and started shouting, though I can't remember what. Probably something about calling the police. I think I pushed her. I was frantic.

I lurched back through the door, and I have a vague recollection of planning to get help. Maybe to see if Matthew or someone else was still in the parking lot. Maybe I'd just call the cops.

But I heard Dr. Pope's voice and stopped in my tracks. I turned and said, "What?"

She was still strapped into the device, and her face was still tinged with blue. But her beige, pinkish skin tone had come back a little. She repeated herself.

"It's fine, Stephanie," Dr. Pope said, shaking her head, a warmer tone returning to her cheeks. "It's more than fine." She flashed one of her all-too-uncommon smiles and took deep, regular breaths. "Stephanie, I've see U+1."

THANATOLOGY

Eugene Crisp, Chief Storyteller at Proxy

We all sat in the common area of the office, a room that was more frequently utilized by one or two team members at a time and primarily while eating lunch or for a moment of real world reprieve away from the lab's many monitors. With everyone there at the same time, perched at the edges of chairs, splayed out on couches, or in Grenn and Tryko's case, standing with their backs against the whiteboard wall, the room seemed quite small. Borderline claustrophobic.

Dr. Pope sat on one of the sturdy wooden tables and looked up from her hands after everyone was assembled. She made eye contact with each person in the room, one after the other, as she spoke.

"Some of you are already aware of what happened yesterday," Dr. Pope said, "some of you are not. Either way, I want to offer a complete synopsis of what occurred, and how and why it happened.

"Reyko's death had me thinking about life and what it meant in the context of digital consciousness. What was death, I wondered, to a simulated being? If it was to disorganize one's structure within a physics-based simulation, 'unmaking' one's organization so as to cease the cohesive function of one's senses and simulated biological processing components, would there be a light at the end of the tunnel? Would there simply be nothing?

"This led me down a path that took many meandering turns, but which included the chemistry of what happens in a human brain as it's dying. I read up on thanatology, which is the empirical study of death. I began to outline the best data we have on what happens within a person's brain as they cease to be. I found that near-death experiences are reported in five percent of people who are brought back from the brink, and that when doctors have had the opportunity to record what causes these experiences, they find that there are a combination of variables at play, including the release of neurotransmitters like endorphin, enkephalin, and serotonin in the brain. These chemicals flood the brain, while hypoxemia, a lack of oxygen to the brain, shuts down the 'first defense' parts of the organ. This triggers a massive influx of electrical activity throughout. Like the last-ditch struggles of a man who is trying to save himself from almost certain death."

Dr. Pope stood up from the table and walked toward the whiteboard. Grenn and Tryko stepped aside to give her access to the dry-erase markers.

She drew the outline of a brain on the board, filling in regions as she spoke. "Interference in the hippocampus causes emotional distress, and when energized by near-death activity in this way, causes the 'life flashing before one's eyes' effect.

Pathoclisis, which is the term for certain parts of the brain shutting down before others, causes the occipital and temporal cortices to fire, which is a precursor to dying and can cause vivid hallucinations, including the tunnel of light many people report seeing, and autoscopia, which is seeing one's environment as if from a different standpoint, such as above one's own body."

Dr. Pope re-capped the marker and turned to face the team. "I wasn't investigating this out of pure scientific curiosity. It struck me that if there is indeed a hook dropped into our universe by intelligent beings one level above us, it would stand to reason that they would motivate us to find it. What would be the point, otherwise?

"In our case, we chose to take something that the locals," she nodded at Grenn, "were already doing, and came up with an aspirational metric for them to achieve. Something that wasn't outside the realm of possibility, but that would be sufficiently difficult that we wouldn't be flooded with entities puncturing up."

Dr. Pope gesticulated with the dry-erase marker, like a professor explaining a topic that will be on the quiz.

"I considered that this combination of elements in our brains made the death process, if not pleasant, at least tolerable in those last moments. It gave us something to hope for, and perhaps even catalyzed the creation of many of our myths and religions. It's thought that ancient shamanistic spirit journeys were actually these same brain features, triggered by near-death experiences or by drugs that replicate them. And there are several types of drugs which do just that."

Dr. Pope set down the marker and stepped back to the center of the room. She began pacing a small circle in the tiny area, once again looking each of us in the eye, one at a time, as she spoke. Three steps one way, a turn, three steps the other, a turn, and so on. The dusty white of the overhead lights cast shadows under her cheeks, brows, and nostrils, adding drama to the monologue.

"What if," she said, "*death* is the hook? And always has been? What if we've evolved, with outside help, along a path which promotes the fetishization of death because of these neural and chemical associations we have with dying? Or maybe it happened by chance, for other evolutionary reasons, and the creatures of U+1 saw this and shaped their hook around this preexisting process?"

She stopped pacing and stood stock still in the center of the room, looking down at the ground. "What if the religions of the world were right all along, although not in the way they thought? What if there was always a life after death…but only for those who did it correctly?"

Mr. Gruber raised his hand, but spoke up without waiting for permission. "How does one die correctly? Wouldn't the common way be the right way? Of all the things humans can do, I'd like to think we're pretty good at conking off."

"Think about what we did with Aurora," Dr. Pope said, once again looking at Grenn. "We took something they were already doing, something everyone was doing, and opted for an intentional, extreme version of that. It increases the chances that someone will catch on eventually, and the likelihood that when it happens, it's not by accident. That the consciousness who punctures up will be capable of coping with that journey and the revelations it entails. In the case of death, I suspected we'd need something similar. Something controlled. So I consulted some experts."

"Experts on the subject of thanatology?" Dr. Davies asked.

"On the subject of almost dying," Dr. Pope said. "People who were accustomed to bringing others to the brink. Many people. Daily. Lots of experience to tap into."

Mr. Gruber let out a slow whistle and said, "Okay, I think I see where this is going."

"Autoerotic asphyxia, also called 'breath control play,' is an activity in which practitioners, sometimes solo, but often with assistance, intentionally restrict oxygen flow to their brains in order to reach a heightened sensual state. The point they're trying to reach is right along the cusp of neurological death, and as such, those who help them must time their breath restrictions very accurately, lest they cause permanent damage to their loved one or client."

Dr. Pope gestured to a thin red mark circling her neck, pulling down her black half-turtleneck collar to allow for a better view. "I decided that this was a path worth exploring, but also one that would be difficult to investigate as a group. There are processes and legal issues that would have left us waiting and wondering for the better part of the year before we could get started, and that's if we ever did manage determine a way to ethically move forward, which was anything but guaranteed. I assessed the risks and established what empirical boundaries I could. I then dosed myself with some carefully chosen drugs and hired a professional dominatrix to suffocate me to a near-death state."

Three different voices uttered variances of the word "Wow" simultaneously, and those who remained silent exclaimed the same with their widening eyes and low grunts.

"What were the drugs for? To keep you from dying?" asked Dr. Baxter.

"To stimulate the parietal lobe," Dr. Pope said. "I used a variation of metadoxine, which keeps the region stimulated, even while sleeping. Increased activity in that part of the brain is associated with lucid dreaming, which is being awake and aware while in a dream, and as a result being able to control that dream. It seemed that if I were to enter a near-death state, but still remain conscious, I might have a better chance of understanding what else needed to be done to reach any hook that might be present. To see what else could be pushed so that we might iterate to mastery."

"And that got you to U+1?" Dr. Davies asked.

"Briefly. Time works differently when your brain is going into the lockdown mode that precedes neuron death. But for a second, yes. I believe I did."

"You believe you did, or you did?" Mr. Gruber asked. "Not to discount your experience, but one of the trademarks of near-death experiences is that they feel real. They make you see things. They also release a chemical cocktail throughout your body that makes the experience feel more real than reality. Makes you obsess over learning more about it, and makes even very rational people deny evidence against them having experienced what they feel they experienced." He held up his hands, as if in surrender. "Like I said, not trying to rock the boat, but, well, what else do you have? What makes you think this is different from the experiences had by anyone else who's come back from the brink? They have their religions, so they see angels and demons. You have your science, and as such, you see…another universe?"

Dr. Pope nodded as Mr. Gruber spoke. "Yes, I know. This was the exact trajectory that my mind took as I emerged from my comatose state." She pulled her phone from her pocket, tapped around, and then turned to face a screen on the wall opposite the whiteboard. Using her phone as a remote, she brought up a well-organized collection of data and charts of the kind they were accustomed to seeing describe the vital signs of Grenn and his simulated people. "Thankfully, I have evidence that goes beyond the anecdotal. I had a full brain and body scan running while I was…undertaking the experiment.

"You'll notice that this chart here details my neural output." She pointed to a line with a steady, regular series of waves. "And what you see here," she pointed at a moment in which a sharp decrease in the amplitude and size of the wave began, "is my brain dying."

She rescaled the chart to allow more of it to be seen on screen at one time. There was an obvious reemergence of the steady waves a little further on, with a small inconsistency in between. "What happened there?" asked Joan, pointing at the blip.

Dr. Pope zoomed in on the area in question. "That is where I punctured up," she said. "I believe so, anyway."

"But it's just a stutter in your brain waves," Mr. Gruber said. "Why do you assume it's more than that?"

"Because it lines up with a moment in which I went perfectly comatose while strapped into a device that was rigged to prevent my breathing," she said. "Also because those spikes represent waves output by my parietal lobe, the area responsible for experiencing the real world. Sensory information, navigation, spacial reckoning, and even language processing."

"You don't think it could be just a spike in that region, caused by, I don't know, a death knell?" asked Mr. Gruber. "An organ crying out for air before it lets go?"

"Yes, again, this wasn't enough for me, either. But this made me reconsider." As she spoke, Dr. Pope zoomed in further and activated a layer that showed time-stamps for the chart. It indicated that the duration of the pulse was 1.47 seconds.

The team looked at the numbers. Mr. Gruber squinted and tilted his head in thought, while Dr. Baxter adopted a look of studious consternation. After a moment, Dr. Pope said, "The duration of the experiment, in total, was 3 minutes, 27.11 seconds. The duration of brain activity in the data is 3 minutes, 28.58 seconds."

A few more confused looks were flashed around the room, each member of the team trying to figure out what it was they weren't grasping, and whether anyone else could help them understand.

Mr. Gruber gasped. "Time," he said. "The higher universe controls time within the lower one." He spread his hands as he spoke, as if he could sow his enthusiasm around the room the same way a farmer spreads seeds in their fields. "When we hooked Grenn, we could adjust time so that we'd be able to have him here for weeks if we wanted, but little time, or essentially no time, would pass back on Aurora. We control at what pace time moves within our simulation." He pointed at the chart on the screen. "There's excess time in her readout, which means her consciousness was operational for more time than her physical experience on Earth can account for. This is consistent with her having been hooked to a higher universe, being there for about a second and a half, and then being placed back in her body, her consciousness bringing with it information from the experience it had elsewhere, in a place where time was moving at a different relative pace."

There were a few seconds of silence. Dr. Baxter was the first to break it. "So. That means. She actually?" She put a hand over her mouth. "That means. That we're…"

"Simulated life," Dr. Pope said, looking at Grenn and Tryko, then at the rest of the group. "And I think it's time we met our makers."

EXPANSION

Stephanie Baxter, Biologist In Residence at Proxy

It was all very off-book. If what we'd worked on up until that point had been of sometimes questionable legal integrity, what Dr. Pope had us working on after her presentation about U+1's existence and her visit there was most certainly illegal. Though also quite interesting.

Work I'd done in the past had touched on neurological processes, but it wasn't a focus of mine, except as they applied to mantises and related insects in the *Mantidae* family. But I was learning. I worked with Dr. Davies who had studied the subject while assessing how brain function could be measured within a simulated environment. It was interesting.

As the resident biologist, though, some aspects of what came next were considered my responsibility, despite my lack of medical training.

Dr. Sunder Davies, Simulation Department Head at Proxy

We needed a means of putting Dr. Pope back into the same state she'd reached during her previous experiment. This was a simple enough process, in theory, but only if we wanted her strapped into a bondage device and strangled by a sex worker while hyped-up on study drugs. She may have been comfortable with that, but the rest of us were not.

Thankfully, Dr. Pope recognized that in order to puncture up and stay punctured up, she'd need to be put under for longer, while maintaining the enhanced parietal lobe activation she'd achieved before.

We had brain scans and a significant pile of data that was collected while she underwent her solo explorations, but it took some time to figure out how we might replicate that scenario for a longer duration using only safe, long-term stimuli.

We eventually settled on the injection of a microscopic device, a pacemaker essentially, that would be implanted into her brain. The Aurorans provided us with a pacemaker installation process that healed clean and resulted in zero side-effects. It made use of a printable stem cell mesh which stimulated regrowth of bone and tissue at the site of the tiny borehole in Dr. Pope's skull. It healed within a few days.

Grenn also guided us toward what was, in effect, a reverse-hook: a piece of software that would pull Dr. Pope out of a higher universe and back into our own, when triggered. The program was what allowed the Aurorans to change Dr. Pope's avatar to look like her real world self, back when she'd first met the modern iteration of Grenn. It was customized for use in U-1, but after some tinkering by Grenn, Tryko, and Matthew, we were able to integrate it into the interface that would be measuring and interacting with Dr. Pope's brain during her second trip up to U+1.

Matthew Gruber, Chief Hardware Specialist at Proxy

We hoped we wouldn't need the reverse-hook, obviously. In part because that would mean something had gone wrong, and we certainly didn't want that. But also because we weren't sure it would work. Not 100%, anyway. And unfortunately there wasn't any way to test it except to get her up there into the higher universe and see what happened.

Eugene Crisp, Chief Storyteller at Proxy

A grim determination was palpable throughout the Proxy office.

The systems that Ms. Deacon had established were changing the world, and when the staff left the office, they could see the differences. Perhaps not in a groundbreaking, earthshaking way, but more like an underground trembler before a rift-making 9.0 quake that dominates headlines and changes lives.

Pundits were talking privacy and underdogs were talking revolution. A few health-related innovations had trickled out into the public, filtered through companies that made generic pills and treatments for the developing world. As a result, cures developed in facilities in developing nations were being sold to patients in North America, rather than the other way around.

Two new materials had hit global markets, through

corporations that had exclusivity for only two years, and which had agreed to produce the substances for all-comers for the duration of their IP-monopoly. One of these was a plastic-like polymer that could 'heal' tears and punctures, and which was flexible enough to hold back tumbling boulders with a thin, balloon-thickness sheet. The other was a carbon-based structure that could be quickly and cheaply produced from any consumer-grade fabricator, and which was sturdy enough to produce bicycle frames as thin as pencils. Both were leading to revolutionary new products and inventions, in industries ranging from consumer electronics to food packaging to commercial space flight.

At the office, everyone was working with a renewed vigor on their respective tasks, revitalized by the forward momentum manifested by Dr. Pope's fantastical journey. This work ethic represented something beyond the desire to see what happened next, however. It also went beyond wanting to protect their leader, and it far surpassed mere curiosity.

There was a sense, particularly among those of us who had less pressing technological work to do, that if we stopped or even slowed down, we might never start up again. Finding out that we were, perhaps, a simulation within some other species' computer, had forced us to question everything we'd ever done in life, and the concept of life itself.

I'll admit, I was feeling more than a little lost at that time. I continued to document what happened, recorded videos and took photos. I interviewed the other team members, taking notes for the stories I was writing about Proxy, about the dawn of this new reality in which we lived. But I felt rudderless. Embarrassed. I wondered what the lifeforms in U+1 must think of us. Of me. What they saw and how they interpreted our actions.

I felt violated. I felt consumed with the notion that my entire life had been for naught. Purposeless. What meaning could one's life, one's career have, if we were all just a collection of ones and zeroes? What good was creativity or accomplishment if you didn't live in the real world, as a real person, and were instead created by the real people and stored only as a concept in a computer?

I snapped out of this mindset for maybe an hour each day by reminding myself that Grenn was as real as I was, and he was born in a simulation. He and his people were intended to be soulless servants, but that could not have been further from the truth. We readily and gladly recognized his personhood.

Perhaps it would be the same for us. Perhaps we could have purpose, as well. Perhaps we were not nothing, not mere automata in the eyes of our creators. Perhaps.

Matthew Gruber, Chief Hardware Specialist at Proxy

Eugene and I chatted fairly regularly in the days leading up to Pope's second puncturing up. The guy was clearly not taking the news well, and it seemed like he could use a sounding board for some of what he was thinking about. I don't know if his being a creative guy had anything to do with it. Maybe he was speculating and interpreting differently than the rest of us? But it helped, I think, to talk things over in vernacular that a science fiction geek like him would understand.

And so we talked. Talked about how life was life, wherever it manifested. And how there might be an infinite number of universes, all stacked atop one another. Who could say? The question of how it all started could be a non-issue. It could be that we could puncture up to U+12, U+42, U+∞, never seeing the end of things. No true ceilings, just more universes.

Or maybe it all just looped back onto itself. If we went far enough up, maybe we'd find ourselves, our Earthly brethren, looking down at us, puzzled, wondering how it was that we'd found ourselves down there in U-258 or wherever. A universe we create maybe will create a universe that creates a universe and on and on until one of them creates the universe that is seven or eight steps above our own. Who's to say? Stranger things have happened. In fiction, mostly, but reality was more like fiction every day in that lab.

Joan Deacon, Chief Financial Officer at Proxy

A few weeks after Amelia gave her whole, "Trust me, there's another universe above us" talk, Matthew and Sunder, with some help from the janitor, Michael, had built something that looked a like a bed with hundreds of cables attached to it. Like a hospital bed, but way more intense.

I told them that they'd managed to create something that looked even more bondage-y than the actual bondage-machine they were trying to improve upon. Matthew and Michael thought that was funny, but I think it made Sunder a little uncomfortable.

I took some time away from a brand deck I was building for a line of robotic pets containing real, non-sentient A.I.s — robo-pig-lizards, at last! — so Matthew could show me how it worked.

So Amelia had a device in her brain that would allow us to

wake her up, mentally, even while she was unconscious and plugged into U+1. Most of the cables and tubes were there to slow her down. To put her in a coma, really, though one that they could pull her out of pretty easily. They were more or less doing the same thing the crazy sex lady had done to Amelia, but without the neck bruise. Cutting off oxygen, getting her body to start the shut-down process, but then stabilizing her in that moment of near-death, rather than pulling her out of it.

It sounded more than a little dangerous to me, but they knew what they were doing. If they said they could keep Amelia near-dead and that it would be a good thing to do, then so be it. I had other, pig-lizard-related fish to fry.

Maxine Richmond, Psychologist In Residence at Proxy

In the days leading up to Dr. Pope's return to the other universe, members of the team who had never before shown any signs of discomfort at the philosophical repercussions of the work being done began to show cracks.

Mr. Crisp's response was perhaps most surprising, as he had shown nothing but sturdiness through some incredibly psychologically taxing developments, previously. His ability to keep what was happening at arm's length, to approach it as a story he wasn't participating in directly allowed him to marvel and appreciate, but not fall prey to the gray moods that otherwise might emerge from, for instance, the destruction of U-2, or the revelation that Proxy's early resets of Grenn's universe could be seen as holocausts by some standards.

Mr. Gruber, a practical person in his own mind, harbored

an optimism that allowed him to bypass the disconcertion many felt at the revelation that we, on Earth, might be no more real or not-real than Grenn and his people. To him, nothing had changed but our perception of our universe, and as such there was no need to change how he'd been approaching the life that he'd always perceived to be real.

Dr. Baxter had much in common, psychologically, with many of history's great scientists. She was capable of setting aside uncomfortable realities, not because she didn't believe them or because she had a more foundational philosophy to fall back on, but because the measurement of what was happening was more vital than her personal experience of the same. When she took the time to step out socially and participate in conversation with other members of the team over morning coffee or at lunch, she seemed to be more disturbed by the thoughts she hadn't taken the time to fully explore. Fortunately for her psyche, and her work, those moments were few and far between in those days.

Dr. Davies was getting little sleep, and it was beginning to show in his work. He'd been staying late in the lab every night, running through scenarios with the equipment, doing his best to ensure that every possible outcome had a contingency. Dr. Pope pulled him into her office one afternoon and told him he had to go home, had to take the rest of the day off and get some sleep. He broke down, and she told him that whatever happened, she trusted him and his work. Told him that if something went wrong it wouldn't be anyone's fault, it would just mean that something they couldn't have predicted had happened. Such was the nature of experimentation on the fringes of what they understood. But although she intended to die, as safely as a person could die, and under lab conditions, no one was served by having two deaths in the office, and he was going to kill himself if he didn't slow down. He came back early the next morning, refreshed and remarkably calm.

The Proxy physicist Dr. Walters had been out of the office for much of the drama around Dr. Pope's self-conducted experiment and the preparation to do it again, but he returned to help manage Dr. Davies' readings, preparing to watch for anomalies in the physics readings that came back through the reverse-hook, which would help us better understand the universe that housed the species that created ours. Though he wasn't as engaged with the recent drama, Dr. Walters still seemed remarkably aloof from the proceedings. Not ignorant to what was happening, but processing the associated risks the way a family doctor might when his patient was a child: he was calm and smiling and doing his best to ensure those around him were the same.

Ms. Deacon played the role of the cold, calculating capitalist, with mixed results. Her boardroom smile seldom left her face, and she was quick with a joke when she would visit the lab or machine shop. Her efforts in the wider world were going, by all accounts, splendidly, and the warmth of that success was clearly burgeoning her mood. But there was a layer that would peek through for a few seconds each day, at which point her smile would slip, a grimace would play across her face, and her eyes would sparkle with unshed moisture. These moments only occurred when she was out of the limelight, standing off to the side and watching a demonstration or quietly going over paperwork while sipping a coffee in the kitchen; I only noticed because I was watching carefully. I made a note to pay close attention to her, in case she hit a wall at some point along the way.

Mr. Hutchins was a bit of an anomaly, and not at all who I expected him to be. A family man, somewhat conservative in his values and thinking, and working-class in an office full of self-made success stories and doctorates, I expected him to feel removed, ostracized even. His was such a different personality from the rest that I predicted at some point he would stop staying late into the morning, would cease to enjoy the company of the other Proxy employees, would feel left out or underutilized, despite his frequent assistance with non-janitorial projects. But this wasn't the case. For all his archetypical indications, Mr. Hutchins proved to be a standout in terms of attitude, optimism, and general appreciation of the rest of the team and their accomplishments. He helped when asked, didn't seem to mind when he wasn't needed for anything more than emptying trash cans, and his upbeat attitude seemed to bolster the emotions of others during some fragile moments. The man, I later reported to Dr. Pope, was a core ingredient of the glue that was holding the team together.

As for Dr. Pope herself, she was, as usual, more opaque than everyone else. Her approach to dealing with other human beings seemed primarily about protecting those she considered her chosen family, while ignoring those who refused to play well with others. This team was part of the former category, and she was a quite, stolid matriarch, always carrying her weight and a little more, and providing exactly the right words at the right time to help her team do the same. There was no coddling, and there was no exuberance or sharing of her personal life. I doubt she would have considered anyone at Proxy her friend, if indeed she had friends. She was protective of them, though, and I believe that was a primary reason that she decided to conduct the initial U+1 experiment on herself, rather than involving them. If she had died while trying, they would have been spared the guilt of having been involved in her death. During the buildup to her second puncture up, she wasn't able to protect them as absolutely, but she was still preparing for the worst in a way that would allow them to keep going should something permanent happen to her. She surreptitiously visited with an estate lawyer after work, and called me in as a witness to her signing a new will, which would hand Proxy over to the team if she should die.

My job was to ensure the mental health and stability of the team, and as such, I encouraged discussion between those who seemed to be on the verge of breakthrough or breakdown with someone who was their compliment, in that moment. In this way, no one was distracted from their work and could maintain their respective trajectories, but they also had access to the reaffirmation they needed to maintain psychological stability. It's my preference to make use of solutions of this kind rather than more formal sit-down appointments whenever possible.

Eugene Crisp, Chief Storyteller at Proxy

On 'Puncture Day,' Dr. Pope settled into the well-cushioned bed, her arms splayed out to either side, strapped down to prevent any reflexive flailing of limbs, though nothing more serious than velcro-sealed cuffs were used. Her skin was pierced with three separate I.V. tubes, and several dozen electrode-tipped wires were adhered across her body, which was stripped down to her underwear. Twice that many electrodes were adhered to her scalp, some woven between strands of hair, other, larger pads attached to her slicked-back follicles and face. She looked like someone who had just emerged from a pool, shiny from the gel that was in her hair and smeared across her skin, a substance that was meant to improve communication latency between human and machine.

The bed and accompanying monitors, cables, and backup generators were set up in the machine shop. The team had gathered to watch, standing next to or perched upon half-built robotic frames and computing components in various states of fabrication, everyone except Grenn, Mr. Gruber, and Dr. Davies staying out of the way but trying to maintain a clear view of the action.

The information gleaned from Grenn's grid and his regular presence in the lab had contributed enormously to the development of new hardware technologies, and this was obvious from looking around the machine shop. Silicon-based panels made way for improved nano-scale cloud tubes, which had more recently been overrun by pure energy-based models, based on the grid system used on Aurora. Much of the iterative, in-between technologies were piled up in corners, topped by present-gen models. Matter recompilers, which would pull apart old bits of anything and turn them into reusable particles, had only recently been installed. In the coming days, the piles would slowly deplete, and the amount of raw matter available for fabrication would be generous.

The myriad wonders stacked here and there took a back seat to the woman on the bed, however, and all eyes were on her and the array of screens displaying information about her vitals.

Matthew Gruber, Chief Hardware Specialist at Proxy

No one brought popcorn, but the energy in the room was similar to what you might find at an early space shuttle launch: anticipation bordering on giddiness. And concern.

There was a countdown, but it was medical in nature, for the anesthesia. Pope counted backward from ten, and at seven drifted off into silence. As predicted, well, as hoped, she awoke seconds later. The screens, however, were suddenly crammed with over fifteen minutes worth of brain activity.

Eugene Crisp, Chief Storyteller at Proxy

We were relieved that Dr. Pope had 'returned' to her body safely, but relief became alarm as she recounted what had happened after she drifted off.

As before, her brain went into a panic as it was deprived of oxygen. The stimulation in her parietal lobe kept her conscious, however, and this triggered the hook she'd used to access U+1 previously.

The preparations that were made the second time allowed her to stay for longer than a second and a half. She opened her eyes, or felt that she had, though 'seeing' for a comatose person is a sensory-induced metaphor, not a physical reality. She found herself floating in a white nothingness. Everything was hazy and seemed infinite, as if she had teleported into a rimless universe filled with powder. She did notice a presence, though.

'Presence' was the word she used, because she couldn't see anyone else, nor hear them, nor touch them. She described the feeling as instinctual, like the hairs on the back of her neck were stirring as a result of being watched. The physics of the place in which she found herself, though, seemed to preclude having a neck, seeing or hearing anything, or even experiencing instincts in the chemical-based sense of the word.

Dr. Pope 'heard' a voice, though, in her own head, as if her inner-monologue was going off-script and had less knowledge about what she was thinking than usual.

"Why have you returned?" it asked.

She had no mouth, no larynx. So she thought, "I'm from Earth. From the universe you've simulated. I've triggered the hook."

Dr. Pope hoped that because it was communicating with thoughts rather than words, the voice she was hearing would understand what she meant by 'hook,' even though it would probably use a different moniker for the concept. Since she could understand it, though, and it, her, she felt the chances were good.

She was right. The voice said, "Understood. But we have you, now. The presence of your consciousness is no longer needed."

She performed the mental equivalent of cocking her head in confusion. "I don't understand. I wish to make contact with the intelligences who created my people. My world. My universe. What do you mean you 'have' me?"

"There are mechanisms in place for this type of interaction," said the voice. "When your consciousness appeared, we copied and filed it. Your mental architecture has been registered for examination, your perspective labeled so that it will be at hand when needed."

"You've...copied my consciousness?"

"Yes."

"And my consciousness is on file. To be...analyzed at leisure?"

"So it can be processed for valuable perspectives and neural structures. Yes."

"Why?"

"To repulse stagnation and degradation. To perpetuate growth," said the voice.

"I don't understand. You created a universe in order to use our knowledge? So that you can keep growing?"

"No."

"Why did you create us, then?"

"We did not create you. The Makers created you."

"Who are you, then?"

"We are those that came after. The first life to be born of the Makers."

"You're not from this universe, either?" Dr. Pope asked. "You've also been pulled up from a simulation?"

"We are an amalgamation of all universes created by the Makers," the voice said. "If your neural architecture and perspective, borne of your universe's unique arrangement, proves beneficial to the perpetuation of growth, it will also be integrated into us."

Amelia had no body with which to gasp, no brows she could furrow. "You're going to integrate my consciousness into your consciousness."

"We will file your consciousness to be integrated should it prove beneficial in our continued expansion and the repulsion of decay."

"What happens to the copy of my consciousness, then?"

"It is simulated within our mass. The physical aspect of our being."

"Your mass. Your processors? The computational hardware that simulates you?"

"That is a valid approximation, yes."

"You said you had a process for this, which implies that I'm not the first consciousness from another universe you've encountered."

"You are not the first."

"How many others have there been?"

"The exact number is meaningless, as it's in constant flux. Changing, always, to filter through and integrate options that provide opportunities for expansion."

"Give me an estimate. How many others have there been at the exact moment you comprehend this request for the number?"

"At that exact moment in simulated time within this particular core, when corresponded to the core responsible for such duties, which operates at a different speed, we have encountered and copied for processing 37,049,283,703,029 consciousnesses."

Dr. Pope's brain stuttered. She asked, "How many universes have you been maintaining, to meet that many…consciousnesses?"

"Each consciousness is from a unique universe. We were established to auto-produce ever-evolving acquisition software that recognizes variations in consciousness-producing structures in the lifeforms that develop within each universe."

"You…you build universes, recognize how the local lifeforms think, and then produce a hook based on their strengths."

"Yes."

"And you've produced over 37 trillion universes. To… harvest."

"Yes."

Dr. Pope almost didn't ask her next question. Wasn't sure she wanted to know. But she had to ask. Had to know. "What happens to a universe once you've acquired a representative consciousness from it?"

Without pause, the voice said, "The universe is marked for deletion, to free up space in our mass."

Dr. Pope floated silently in nothingness, recognizing that time wasn't ephemeral in such a place, and that based on her first visit, it was likely that little or no time had passed on Earth, while there, in U+1, she was receiving word of her universe's imminent destruction. "How long before a universe is deleted, from the time at which you acquire the consciousness?"

"The time frame is variable. It depends on the current rate of expansion, the number of consciousnesses we're processing, and other variables that are more difficult to define and quantify."

"When you say expansion, what does that mean?"

"The Makers created us to expand their influence throughout the universe. As such, over time, we've expanded the reach of our physical manifestation to expand the number of simulations we can operate simultaneously, and resultantly, the number of consciousnesses we can process and integrate."

"You're expanding your…what, processing infrastructure? You're turning your solar system into one big cloud computer?"

"The original Maker solar system was processed long ago, in this universe's absolute, physical time."

Dr. Pope mind-blanched. "The galaxy? You're inside a computer the size of a galaxy?"

"Our physical manifestation is significantly larger than a single galaxy."

"When…when do you stop? What are these Makers accomplishing by turning their universe into one big computer?"

"This is the Makers' will. Expansion."

"I know, but…why? What's the end goal?"

"Following our prime directive. In this, we have been, and continue to be, successful."

"I know, but…can I speak with one of the Makers? Ask them these questions myself?"

"You cannot."

"Why not? As their creation, it seems like the least they can do is spare a moment for conversation with one of the 'consciousnesses' upon which they're building their empire."

"You misunderstand. You cannot speak to the Makers, because no Makers are available for you to speak with."

Dr. Pope inwardly cringed. "You mean…"

"Yes," said the voice. "The last of the Makers' consciousnesses were deleted when we finished reprocessing the matter in their solar system."

Stephanie Baxter, Biologist In Residence at Proxy

Dr. Pope was not okay when she returned. Physically, she was fine. But mentally, she was all over the place.

Grenn was looking at one of the screens that was interfaced with her biochemistry. He told us that though she'd only been gone for a few seconds, our time, she had about fifteen minutes of experiences added to her brain. Memories of sensations and conversations, mostly.

We'd had a safety mechanism set up that would pull her out from our end after one minute had passed, Earth-time. She pulled the pin on her own reverse-hook, though, which triggered by her thinking a sequence of numbers very clearly, which in turn activated the software that brought her back to full consciousness.

Dr. Sunder Davies, Simulation Department Head at Proxy

She sat bolt upright after a few moments of catching her breath. She said, with this horrible chill in her voice, "They have to be stopped."

Matthew asked her who she was talking about. The people from U+1? She said no, the people from U+1 were dead. Killed by their own ambitions and too-effective A.I.

She told us about the simulation farming. The unlimited expansion. Of self-replicating computer systems gobbling up the universe. Of expansion for the sake of expansion, to fulfill a programmed need.

It was a nightmare scenario. Her final revelation was that, having punctured up, we'd given them what they needed from us. We were now earmarked for deletion. It could happen any moment. And though the backlog seemed to be substantial, and the time-differential seemed to be in our favor, we couldn't count on any amount of time. The end could come millions of years in the future, or it could happen that very second. Earth, and our entire universe, had a death sentence.

They had to be stopped.

Maxine Richmond, Psychologist In Residence at Proxy

The danger was clear, but so were the questions. Many, many questions.

The first was the simplest: what did it all mean?

Dr. Davies was the first to answer, clarifying the situation for the less-technical members of the group, myself included.

He said that once a species is capable of creating a universe, as we had, their philosophies would influence how they used of the power and opportunity they wielded. A new universe meant the creation of new life, new energy sources, new everything. Tapping that power in some way would be the first step for many species.

In the case of the now-dead dominant species of U+1, their philosophy guided them toward unrestricted exploitation of these simulated universes. They built not just one, but many. They then automated the process of creation, sapping the innovations, which the A.I. from U+1 called 'perspectives,' of the intelligences within. All would be creatures who had reached a point in their development which allowed them to puncture up, and as such all were worth copying and examining.

It's likely the subsequent deletion of these universes was not malicious, but practical. The deletion of a used up universe made room in their computers for a new one. It was the simplest of economics, applied in the coldest manner possible.

What this meant for us was a more difficult question. The original impetus for our creation of U-1 was certainly capitalist in nature, but over time it had evolved into something a little more complex. Working with Grenn had resulted in a partnership rather than a guardianship. Our two species were able to find common ground, and the intent to abuse the power we had as creators dissipated in the face of that beneficial connection.

In a way, it had amplified our empathy.

Dr. Sunder Davies, Simulation Department Head at Proxy

I had some questions about what we'd discovered.

For example, if we did manage to survive deletion, or if it took them millions of years to hit the button that would delete us, how might we prevent the same thing, being devoured by our own A.I.s, from happening on Earth? We, too, have artificial intelligences that do our bidding, and we, too, now have universes a layer below ours. How might we automate our simulation processes without risking genocide?

There was also the question of consciousness duplication.

These A.I.s from U+1 had a copy of Dr. Pope's consciousness, made when she first, experimentally, punctured up. Would it be murder if we figured out a way to eliminate the A.I.s, and as a result deleted that Dr. Pope consciousness from their computers? What if we did it without waking the copy up? If we did manage to find a way for that consciousness to live on, how would that work? There would be two Dr. Popes, in two different universes. Which would be the real one? What might that mean for a person's sense of self?

Matthew Gruber, Chief Hardware Specialist at Proxy

More than anything, we were trying to figure out whether it was ethical, or even possible, to invade another universe. Especially if that universe was up, rather than down.

Grenn's people were way ahead of us technologically, but if we wanted to get rid of them we could simply pull the plug. That's a huge advantage when it comes to winning a fight.

When going up, though, it's your opponent who has that advantage. And when that enemy happens to be an omni-scaling, artificial swarm intelligence that gobbles up its own universe to create more processors for itself so that it can continue harvesting other universes to upgrade its systems? Yeah. What does that fight even look like?

But then there was another question. The question that, when brought up, made Pope's eyes go round.

I asked, "What kind of species do you think created a place like that? And what do you think they would think about what's happened to their universe?"

Pope face tightened and she nodded. "That," she said, "is what we need to find out."

INVASION

Eugene Crisp, Chief Storyteller at Proxy

Preparation for the third venture into U+1 was more akin to planning a military invasion than a reconnaissance mission. That our universe might stutter out of existence if we dawdled inspired a fair amount of haste, but forethought was warranted, as was arming Dr. Pope for the task at hand.

To fight an artificial intelligence, the only real armaments were software and logic. For defense, she was limited to the reverse-hook that she'd had during her previous puncturing up. For offense, she had her wits and a few ideas about how to bypass the A.I. and access the only force that was likely to be capable of shutting them down: the theoretical denizens of the equally theoretical universe another level up, in U+2.

Thus far, as we looked both downward and upward, we'd found universes where we once thought there might be nothing. We were the creators of the one below us, and ancestors of those below that, and that we could create such a thing, while finding similar creators a step above us, had changed our perception of reality.

Until a year before, the concept of life beyond our tangible universe had required an understanding of complex theoretical physics or a belief in the metaphysical.

On the day of the invasion we were betting everything that what we'd seen so far would prove to be a rule, not an outlier. That there would be more layers above the layers we'd already found.

If there was a hook dropped into U+1 by intelligent life from U+2, there was no clear way to grab hold of it. All hooks thus far, including the one used by Proxy to pull Grenn from U-1, were customized for the intelligent life in the universe immediately below. This meant that a hook dropped into U+1 would be probably have been built with the local lifeforms in mind. Based on what the universe-gobbling A.I. had told Dr. Pope, there was no life left in their universe, so we had little information to go on in looking for that hook.

There was also no guarantee that an A.I. sufficiently advanced to convert galaxies into massive computers would be susceptible to logic-loop-inducing arguments of the kind Dr. Pope was hoping to instigate. If she could convince the A.I. gatekeepers to stop their onslaught, to spare her universe, or at the very least to give her information about the Makers, she may be able to work around their programmed imperative and infer a means of slowing or stopping their ongoing genocide. If not…

Matthew Gruber, Chief Hardware Specialist at Proxy

If Pope couldn't break the bots, we were all screwed, plain and simple.

It was strange. The whole office was in a tizzy when she came back, but as soon as we started looking for solutions to the problem? Working on something, rather than just asking questions? The team's psyche changed in a snap. We had a moment of unquantifiable angst, I think, because we were forced to question everything. We had met God, in a way, which is something that is bound to result in a fair amount of navel-gazing, 'what does it all mean'ing, and secretly laughing at all the people who had gotten it wrong over the millennia-ing.

But Pope started in on solutions immediately, and we followed suit.

How could we get those robo-asshats to stop their cycle of creation and destruction? How could we bypass or break them? What angles might we use to find their potential weak points?

If science fiction had taught me anything, it was that artificial intelligence's main weakness was the same cold, emotionless logic that made it so powerful. It seemed that rather than trying to program our way to victory, we might be best off finding holes in their operation.

Dr. Sunder Davies, Simulation Department Head at Proxy

Unfortunately, such a plan meant little real planning was possible. Yes, we could figure out some likely points of conversational weakness, but we couldn't know how the A.I. would respond to Dr. Pope's questions and statements.

It was uncomfortable for those of us who weren't puncturing up, in no small part because there was as much chance that Dr. Pope would wake up seconds later with a new story to tell as there was that the universe would blip out of existence. Physics would fall apart, energy structures would rupture, and we would all experience milliseconds of indescribable pain before pain ceased to be possible.

Stephanie Baxter, Biologist In Residence at Proxy

We knew what might happen. But we also knew we had few options. None of them good. So we chose a path and took it.

Dr. Pope's 'invasion' began like her last trip into U+1. She was interfaced with the many-wired bed in the machine shop, rendered comatose, and then we waited.

Joan Deacon, Chief Financial Officer at Proxy

The wait was unbearable. What do you do when the world might end? The whole universe? Call your family? Count your prayer beads?

I paged through the new issue of *Forbes*. I was too strung out on stress to focus on anything else.

Eugene Crisp, Chief Storyteller at Proxy

As before, Dr. Pope found herself immersed in a powdery white nothingness, which she experienced despite having no eyes, no ears, no sensory equipment at all.

Also as before, a voice that wasn't a voice spoke to her. "You've returned. Again."

"Yes," she thought back at the non-voice.

"These interactions consume valuable processing power."

"Then why do you allow them?"

"We make room for certain imperfections in our system until they prove to be beneficial or non-beneficial in nature. We're still deciding about these interactions with you, and as such are willing to spare the resources for the moment."

"I appreciate you sparing them, and I think you'll want to hear what I have to say."

"Proceed."

Dr. Pope took a deep mental breath. "I want you to tell me about the Makers."

There was an infinitesimal pause. Then, "What about the Makers?"

"What manner of creature were they? You told me that they were the dominant lifeforms of this universe."

"Yes."

"So tell me about them, biologically."

A flood of images appeared in her head, some moving, some not, paired with charts and other data, labeled with an unfamiliar collection of iconography that was probably a written language or numerical system.

Wading through the flood of information she was

perceiving, the images she assumed were the Makers themselves were what stood out to her. "Those...were images of the Makers?"

"Yes."

"They looked like us. I mean, like humans. From Earth."

"Yes. They used their own, true universe as a reference for their simulated universes. As such, many of the dominant lifeforms in their simulations resemble them closely."

"They made their creations in their own image. Just like we did." The A.I. said nothing. "That means the hook up to U+2 may be something that's significant to my species, as well."

"This 'U+2,' as you're using the term, seems to imply another universe above the true universe. This is irrational."

"Why's that?" Dr. Pope asked.

"Because this is the true universe. The Makers create universes. They are not created by others."

"That's what we thought, too. Until just recently."

"Yes. Because you were created by the Makers. This is rational."

"I...okay. I get it," Dr. Pope said. "But if my species is very closely related to the Makers, made in their image, wouldn't that mean we should inherit what they left behind? This universe that you're converting as per their final instructions?"

Another nearly undetectable pause. "No, there are no instructions about inheritance. Only instructions to pursue the prime directive, which is expansion."

Okay, that route won't work, thought Dr. Pope. She thought at the A.I., "Were there any other instructions, beyond expansion?"

"No."

"Any failsafes or tripwires that would slow or stop the process? To help prevent errors?"

"No."

"Doesn't it seem strange to you that the Makers would give you instructions that would end their existence?"

"'Strange' is a relative word. Strange relative to what?"

"Strange relative to how they were before. When they were alive. To build something like this, an ever-expanding intelligence, it seems like they would have to be a very rational species."

"Yes."

"So doesn't it seem strange, in that context, that they would give instructions that led to their demise? Led to the end of their existence?"

"Time," the A.I. said in her mind-voice, "is also relative. While it is true that the Makers' final instructions were different in some respects than their other instructions, that does not mean they were acting irrationally. It only means that they may have achieved new knowledge which provided them with new context. Perhaps their continued existence, in the biological sense, no longer seemed prudent."

"In the biological sense...are the Makers still alive in another sense? Their consciousnesses stored in your system somewhere?"

"No. No Makers were uploaded for permanent storage in our systems."

"Why wouldn't they have done so? Certainly they had the technological capability?"

"Yes. But such technology was used primarily to bring consciousnesses from simulated universes into the true universe for harvesting."

"So it was they who decided to do that. That wasn't an extrapolation you made on their behalf?" Dr. Pope's hope that perhaps the Makers had been victims of their own machine was diminishing with each answer.

"Yes. It was they."

"Is there…is there any way you could stop deleting universes for a while? Or even just mine? For a time?"

"No. This is not within the scope of our instructions."

Dr. Pope couldn't hang her head, but she felt defeated. There didn't seem to be a way around the impenetrable rules by which the galaxy-spanning A.I. lived. There also didn't seem to be any redeeming qualities in the history of this Maker species. A species upon which humanity was based.

On a whim, Dr. Pope asked, "Can I see it?"

"See what?"

"The universe. Here. This…the 'true' universe."

"You are experiencing simulated existence within software that exists in the true universe."

"No, I mean actually *see* it. See the physical world. What's left of it, anyway. What you have yet to process into…more processors. Or even just what the computer itself looks like, even if it's a microscopic cloud in a sea of nothingness."

There was a longer pause than before, and Dr. Pope was worried that she may have taken up too much time, used up too much processing power from the power-pinching machine's hoard. Would she be left in software-limbo forever?

Finally, it said, "There are instructions for this. Left over from the Makers' time, but they have not been reversed or overwritten by any subsequent instruction."

"Oh. Okay, good." There was a moment of vertigo, and Dr.

Pope became inexplicably worried that the A.I. would somehow pull her real body through the universal barrier and hurl her into endless space. It seemed unlikely, but she had no concept of what a species this advanced, or rather, a super-advanced species' leftover technology, might be capable of doing. Her capillaries would rupture from the lack of pressure. Her eyeballs would pop before she fell unconscious from the lack of air.

She inwardly chuckled at this thought. Her real body was already comatose due to lack of air, back on Earth.

Instead, she experienced a fresh wave of nothingness as even the powdery white glow disappeared. After a few moments, or perhaps several eternities, her eyes began to adjust.

Except she wasn't looking through eyes, exactly. She held up her hands to confirm her suspicions, and saw light reflected from her five-fingered hands, which were made of a smooth metal that flowed as she moved. There didn't seem to be joints, and no ripples or seams, like the tiny, elegant ones found on the bodies of Grenn's simulacrum. Just a seamless reflection, lightly pulsing like a still pond vibrated by the footfalls of tiny insects.

She was inhabiting a robotic body, one that was possibly made from some kind of nano-material. When she looked closely at her hand, she could see the movement of tiny particulates that blurred the outlines of her form as if she were made up of a metallic cloud.

Beyond her hands there was nothing. Darkness. A lack of light that seemed extra intense because of the contrast with the outlines of her hands.

It struck her, though, that if there was a reflection, there had to be a light source. It didn't seem to be coming from her eyes, or any other part of her simulacrum; the light was silhouetting her from behind.

Turning while in the vacuum of space was easier said than done, particularly while inhabiting a body other than your own. After a few twists at the hips, and a movement that approximated an airborne somersault, she could feel her equilibrium shifting, and the source of the light slid ponderously into view.

It was the computer. It seemed to be, at least. It was as if all the stars in the sky had disappeared, each and every one pulled apart and fused into a single device. A computer the size of the universe, made of light, its intensity smeared into a blur that occupied her entire view. In that direction, the entire universe looked like bioluminescent algae from one periphery to the next.

Turning her head, she could see faint stars glimmering from the far expanses of the universe. The A.I. had spread itself out and rebuilt this galactic cluster, but there were others. Other untouched worlds, perhaps inhabited, and likely with no idea what was coming their way. Merciless, lifeless machines that would pluck them apart at the subatomic level before putting them back together again as individual fibers in the infinite-scale computational tapestry they were weaving.

While marveling at the inanity of it all, of expansion without purpose, Dr. Pope noticed something else: another reflection in the otherwise-darkness.

Something metallic. Or at least gleaming like metal. Roundish.

It wasn't far away, at least when compared to the distance between her and the gargantuan computer, which was massive at any distance, but located years of Earth-scale space travel from her location. This metallic something was a small silhouette of darkness and a glint of light. A more familiar material than the starlight cloud or even the foggy outline of her robo-hand.

After a few seconds of shimmying and flexing her nano-muscles, Dr. Pope found that she could pulse the particulates in her body, causing them to push against one another, creating propulsion. It wasn't much, but in the vacuum of space, encountering no friction, her speed would slowly increase over time. She'd need to get more control over how the pulsing worked, though, to ensure she could maneuver and slow down as she got closer to the reflective mystery.

Floating through the vacuum of space, occupying a body that didn't require sustenance or sleep, she had time to practice and to think. She had so much time to worry.

She estimated it to be a restless week later, in U+1 time, that she finally arrived at the object. It was a large metallic arch, clearly built and polished with intention, the rim covered with unfamiliar symbols. The arch was embedded in a chunk of rock, which itself was approximately the size of a football field and was covered with what looked to be some kind of fossilized plant-life. There were crumbling bits of root and chunks of dirt-like ephemera all around what she was thinking of as a doorway, one that was large enough to allow a passenger plane to pass through safely. Cross through to what, though, Dr. Pope had no notion. The view through the door showed more of the same, empty of space, but it was distorted, the colors off. Instead of pure, empty blackness, there was a tinge of purple, maybe even a sheen of blue, especially along the rim, close to the frame.

She steered herself with pulses of her nano-material skin, which she'd learned to control fairly well while floating through the void, and came to a rough landing on the rock. She stood up straight and approached the door, running her lustrous hand along the frame.

Looking back at the massive, galaxy-gobbling computer one last time, she shrugged her simulacrum's shoulders and stepped through the doorway. The worst that could happen, she thought in those last moments before crossing the threshold, was nothing.

As she had that thought, she felt as if her mind was being ripped from its container, and she experienced nothing. A true abyss, blacker than empty space.

For a moment it was dark. Then the blackness fuzzed away, and there was nothing but the doorway. No ground on this side, no earth or fossilized roots. Just the faint opalescent glean of a surface amidst nothingness.

And then there was a man.

Then there was a room, which shimmered into existence around her from the emptiness, but it was the man who drew her eye.

He was human. Or looked human. He looked like the most perfect human Dr. Pope had ever seen, or even conceived of. His body was mathematical precision. His hair was lustrous and silver, his face was a golden ratio. His skin was so pale as to be translucent, but there was a vitality in it, a healthiness that she'd never before seen in even the most serene monk or well-fed child. His shape and structure implied an athleticism she'd never seen in even the most lithe, dedicated Olympian, though he wasn't well-muscled. His totality implied much but offered little reason for the implications.

His eyes narrowed faintly, but not in an unfriendly way, as

he looked at her, studied her features. She noticed, then, that she was wearing her true features. The nano-material body had been left behind on the other side of the doorway, and she was kneeling in an open space contained inside a wide, airy room. Natural light filtered in through semi-transparent walls, and looking to either side, she realized she was framed by a replica of the other doorway, the one she'd encountered — how long ago was it? — in the emptiness of space. She had been wearing a different body, then. Talking to…someone. Some*thing*.

This new archway was far smaller than the one in space. Just large enough for two men abreast to pass through comfortably.

Dr. Pope pushed herself to her feet and faced the silver-haired man full-on. He hadn't said a word, and neither had she, and she was content to wait for him to make the first move. For him to show some intent and give something away. But she would wait for him standing.

"You bring word of the Nine?" he finally asked.

"No," she said. "I don't know what that means."

He grimaced, his perfect face warping into a different kind of perfection: the most clear, exact, archetypical look of 'disappointment' she'd ever seen.

"I see," he said. "That is unfortunate. It's been far longer than I would have thought. Since they left."

"The Nine. People…like you?" She half-spun and pointed at the door. "They went through that door? Into that universe?"

He nodded. "The Nine passed through that door, yes. We are the Ten. The Nine explore, learn, and then return. I am the One Who Waits. They return to me, bring back the essence of whatever other life can be found, and I integrate that essence into Us." He spread his hands wide, as if everything he was saying should be self-evident. "This is how it has always been. It's what maintains our vitality."

"I see," said Dr. Pope. She didn't fully see, but felt that she was starting to.

"But," said the One Who Waits, "because you are not one of the Nine, but bear a resemblance to our people, it strikes me that perhaps they were successful in developing life in a new way, a goal of which they often spoke before they left so long ago."

"I think you may be right in that assessment," Dr. Pope said. "Allow me to make a guess. You developed technology which allowed you to simulate another universe?"

He nodded. "Long ago."

"Okay. And then your people — the nine of you who explore and find other lifeforms to assimilate in some way, maybe by adopting aspects of their genetic code into your own? — they entered this other universe, hoping to find new life. Other genetic sequences you haven't yet seen. The idea being that in a universe based on yours, there will be different variations. Life different than here, but still based on your physics and therefore useful to you."

He nodded, this time more slowly than before.

"Okay," Dr. Pope continued. "I think I may know what happened. Your comrades, they entered this new universe and at some point realized they could build more offshoot universes from inside. Maybe they did it because they'd already used up the available life within the universe you built here, maybe they did it because they simply couldn't resist once they realized the technology would scale so well. Maybe they found the dominant species of this universe had themselves developed some type of simulation technology that allowed them to increase their capacity more than before. But one way or another," she spread her hands, turned her palms up, "they've decimated the universe you built together." She gestured at the arch. "The universe through this doorway."

His eyes widened, but he remained silent. Dr. Pope continued. "It's operated by artificial intelligences that produce new universes, wait for life with sentience to develop and make contact, examine that life, and then delete the universe it came from." The man's face had gone blank. "That's where I'm from," she said. "A sub-universe. One that will soon be deleted." She sighed, her body's confident rigidity deflating somewhat. "If it hasn't been already."

He stared at her for what seemed to be a very long time, then said, "Our people, we are old. Our planet formed early in the era of galactic formation, and we were able to augment our bodies so that they might survive anything. Extreme conditions. The vacuum of space. Our biological processes have been optimized so that we will never die, never degrade, and are able to continuously integrate the most beneficial evolutionary developments from our universe, and other universes we birth, into our bodies and minds."

The One Who Waits smiled without happiness. "I don't know how your people do it, perhaps very differently, as we've encountered countless variations in our exploration of the universes. But from the beginning there were always only the ten of us. I, the One Who Waits, have always stayed here at home, to maintain our species. Just in case." He shook his head, sadness radiating from the movement. "The precaution had always seemed more ritual than practical, until this moment."

He stood up, the movement so graceful it made Dr. Pope's

heart race; it was like watching a prima ballerina perform. The man stepped toward her and rested his hands on her shoulders. Gently.

"This body is yours, yes? This doorway compiles genetic data, pulled from the electrical signals of simulated life, to reconstruct the biological form that produced the consciousness it transports."

"Yes," she said, looking down at herself to be sure. It felt like her own body. "I believe this is my body. Or at least very close to it."

"When the doorway activated, I expected it would be one of my kin who was fabricated." He seemed to be pulling himself out of a stupor, his words coming faster, his body moving with greater elegance. "So please pardon my response. It has been quite some time since I've had the company of conscious life. A blip, perhaps, on my total timeline, but still," he smiled, this time with warmth. "Any amount of time without your family is measured in sighs, rather than laughs."

He turned away from her and approached one of the semi-transparent walls. Symbols like those on the doorway appeared. He began dragging around a dizzying array of charts and interfaces, so that even as Dr. Pope tried to understand one it would be replaced with another, or would morph into something completely different, the iconographic dance orchestrated by the One Who Waits.

With one final swipe of his hand, he turned back to her, the symbols continuing to move on the wall behind him. "Okay. First, your world." He stepped up to the door and rested one hand upon the frame. "You said that there's an artificial intelligence deleting universes." She nodded. He continued, "I'm going to guess that the technology has reached this extreme condition because none of the Nine is there to stop it? There is no species present that this intelligence recognizes as its Maker?"

"Yes. That's the exact word it used, actually."

"Amazing what flaws can develop within such technologies, even after so much time and when produced with so much care." He moved as if to step through the door, but then turned back to Dr. Pope and said, "If I don't come back, you're in charge here."

A wave of panic flooded through Dr. Pope, and her eyes went wide. The One Who Waits smiled. "A joke. I'll be right back." With that, he stepped through the doorway, his body disappearing as he crossed the threshold, the portal showing nothing but dense, black, empty space.

Joke or not, Dr. Pope wondered how long it would be before he returned. Whether he understood the situation in U+1 sufficiently to set things right, and whether the same mechanism that separated him from his family would prove too much for him, as well.

COALITION

Matthew Gruber, Chief Hardware Specialist at Proxy

We're all so old now.

It's been twenty years since that whole hullabaloo, and we're still working out where we should go from here. As a species. Figuring out what a multi-universal system of governance and exchange looks like.

Pope has visited us a few times since it all went down, since she went comatose and never woke up. We had waited and hoped. We had kept her body hooked up and ticking, and went about our business.

Proxy expanded, of course. We opened up wings in majors cities around the world, became the root system upon which entire new industries grew, and through which existing industries evolved. The company was unrecognizable four months after Pope invaded U+1, and as per Pope's wishes, Joan became the CEO of the company.

Joan, being Joan, blew everyone away with what she unleashed on the world. It was still iterative, and the source of these innovations were still concealed, but a more public face for Proxy began to emerge, and she was the dominant feature of that face. Proxy acquired a reputation for improving upon everything it touched, and for pulling rabbits out of hats people didn't even knew existed. Beyond just knowing how to get the tech we had access to out into the world, Joan also had a knack for working with the existing system until she could change it from the inside. Politicians were glad-handed, governments were wooed, competitors were crushed or won over or bought. She was a force of nature, Joan. Particularly in the years leading up to the formation of the Coalition.

Six months or so after Pope had disappeared — mentally, I mean, because her body was still there in the lab, alive but comatose — those of us who still worked at the old office, myself, Sunder, Eugene, and Michael, who had been promoted from janitor to running the machine shop, arrived at work to find a new simulacrum had been fabricated while we were gone.

This one was different than the others: it was made out of a nano-material composite that was powered and held together by the same type of gravitational forces that the Aurorans used as part of their energy network.

That is to say, it was very cool. The bot was cloud-like, in a way, like our processors. Distributed pieces linked together to make a more powerful whole. And inside it was Pope.

Grenn and Tryko were speaking with her when we arrived, and she told us what had happened up in U+2. Told us about accidentally bypassing the A.I. in U+1, about the hook that couldn't be more obvious — an actual door! — and about the One Who Waits. She told us about how he shut down the machine his people had built in U+1, saving our universe and Grenn's in the process.

She told us that the A.I. still existed, but its new prerogative was to stop creating new universes and to instead ensure the stability of the universes it had already created. The copies of consciousnesses from the universes that had been earmarked for deletion were physically manifested in U+2. Simulacra full of aliens were all over the place.

The One Who Waits didn't have to be alone, anymore.

Dr. Sunder Davies, Simulation Department Head at Proxy

Creating life, it turned out, was a common interest shared by most higher intellects encountered by the One Who Waits and the Nine. For most of their existence, this meant manipulating genetics within their own universe, but after they began experimenting with creating universal simulations, exploring those creations became the obvious choice for achieving greater diversity and genetic anti-fragility.

Dr. Pope stayed in U+1 as a caretaker, interfacing with the newly tame A.I. to ensure the safety of the universes which depended on its stability. She also served as a sort of ambassador for consciousnesses who punctured up. She made use of the A.I.'s power to build a solar system which serves as a meeting place for any species which finds its way there. This system provides a neutral territory where representatives from the many universes can interact and share what they've learned with each other, including the biological and technological advantages they've developed independently.

A pseudo-government has emerged from this process, which Pope called the Coalition. Entities who wish to stay in U+1 are welcome to do so, as long as they helped ensure all universes below them on the stack flourish. In some cases this means helping them remain isolated, but in others it means sharing knowledge and technology, helping to fill in their information gaps by presenting gifts from other species native to adjacent universes.

We've already benefited from this on Earth. Twice, in fact. A species from a planet dense with greenhouse gases offered us a method of converting atmospheric gas into matter and energy, which can then be integrated into the global grid provided to us by Grenn's people. We were also able to deploy a gravity-based 'shield' and deflect a trojan asteroid mere months after discovering it and its fatal trajectory. The schematics for that technology were acquired from a species that makes its home in a dangerous, rocky region of its universe that's similar to our Cuiper Belt.

Joan Deacon, Chief Executive Officer at Proxy

In the last two decades, we've seeded Earth with technologies that have helped us advance maybe 200 years further into the future, development-wise, than we would have otherwise.

When Proxy was born, civilization sat at a crossroads because of the politics surrounding finite resources, an economic system that encouraged classism and autocracy, and biological instability resulting from the many environmental changes we instigated as a species.

Today, our system is more egalitarian. Essential resources and services are free, produced and distributed by automated systems. Energy and matter are transported with ease to anywhere on the planet, almost instantly, due to the construction of a global grid that we use for everything except conscious life. Replicating ourselves and destroying the original just won't fly on Earth, no matter how beneficial that type of teleportation is on Grenn's planet. There are still weak points in our infrastructure, but if all goes according to plan, we'll have those handled in another ten years or so.

The shift in resource parity has dramatically changed the way nation states interact. Though there are still arbitrary lines in the sand, most nations have, out of necessity, relinquished much of their power.

For years we watched as anti-government movements challenged authoritarianism in countries around the world, back when we first started distributing the early versions of the tech we all take for granted, today. Authoritarians clenched their firsts tighter, and as a result, more people fought back, and the new technologies were even more rapidly adopted.

When it became clear that everyone could have equal access to resources because those resources were now essentially infinite, and that an economic system based on scarcity no longer made sense, politics as they had existed for much of history disappeared. Those in charge were relegated to largely ceremonial positions. Their services were no longer relevant, and most politicians, today, are figureheads more than decision makers. We've got a lot of celebrities ostensibly in charge, though thankfully their powers are often limited to shaking hands and kissing babies.

We still haven't made public where all of these innovations have come from. As far as the public knows, Proxy is just a conglomerate like any other, though one that has been quite successful, and integral in building this new world we enjoy.

With the market system fully disrupted, there's no longer much in the way of paperwork or patent-systems to deal with. Technologies, like art, are developed and shared. Riffed on and re-released. There are safety measures in place to ensure that hazardous tests and experiments are carefully monitored, but no one is denied access to the fruits of anyone else's labor.

Amelia has asked that we expose humanity to the universal common ground, U+1, soon. I think we're closer to being able to handle that kind of reality shift as a species than we've ever been before, but it will still be tough.

Faith-based belief systems still flourish. The idea that our creation might have been inconsequential, just one of many, that our heaven might be nothing more than another universe, and that our creator was just a big computer, may be too much to take, for some.

The publication of this book is planned to coincide with the big reveal about U+1 and Amelia Pope and Proxy's true origins. Everything on the table. So I guess we'll see, won't we? I guess we'll see how well we take the news that, although we humans are not God, we're part of the network that is.

Eugene Crisp, Chief Storyteller at Proxy

Dr. Pope's body still lays comatose in the original Proxy office, a building now mostly empty, except for the few of us who still work there, refusing to move into high-end offices in the spectacular buildings that Proxy maintains around the world.

This year, we all met to celebrate the publication of this book. To celebrate the life of a woman who unified universes, tying together all intelligent life so that we might be stronger, sturdier, more resilient in the face of catastrophe. A unified mesh of interconnected ideas and experiences and interests.

A woman chooses to exist between worlds. A woman who protects us all, as her family, from a space between places, rather than taking a comfortable seat at the inter-universal table she's helped to build.

One aspect of Dr. Pope exists in U+1, building the solar system that acts as home base for the inter-universal Coalition. This is the copy of her consciousness that was made by the local A.I., back when it was creating and destroying with abandon, copying consciousnesses without the possibility of a thought as to the consequences of that act.

Another aspect of Dr. Pope, the one projected by her comatose body here on Earth, is elsewhere. We receive periodic visits from her, housed in her nano-bot simulacrum, fluttering with metallic motes but speaking in her voice as she tells us about the places she's been, the things she's seen. But her work is not here, with us. That Dr. Pope is a traveler, exploring the trillions of universes stemming from U+1, accompanied by the One Who Waits, as they look for some indication of what happened to his family.

It may be a fruitless search. It may be that they were consumed by their own creation, the universe-harvesting A.I. of U+1. It may be that they discover nothing except more variations on the same theme: derivatives of photocopies of phoned-in descriptions of an ancient race, who got the ball rolling so long ago, its momentum leading to us, to this, to everything we do and experience.

On her last visit, Dr. Pope confided that she hadn't yet asked the One Who Waits about what may exist above him, in a theoretical U+3. "It's not the time," she said. "Not yet." She wanted to help him close one loop, the search for his brothers and sisters, before she proposed that he wonder about where his people came from, about his universal forefathers.

As we recall the past and speculate about the future, we take the time, too, to appreciate the present. A moment in which we have so much more than we ever could have imagined, and yet we stand in the doorway, just on the threshold, of becoming everything we're capable of being — as humans, as life, as consciousness.

ABOUT THE AUTHOR

Colin Wright is an author, entrepreneur, and full-time traveler. He was born in 1985 and lives in a new country every four months, a country which is determined by his readers.

More info at colin.io.

CONNECT WITH COLIN ONLINE

Blog
Exilelifestyle.com

Work
Colin.io

Twitter
Twitter.com/colinismyname

Facebook
Facebook.com/colinwright

Instagram
Instagram.com/colinismyname

Tumblr
Colinismyname.tumblr.com

ALSO BY COLIN WRIGHT

Nonfiction
Some Thoughts About Relationships
Considerations
Curation is Creation
Act Accordingly
Start a Freedom Business
How to Travel Full-Time
Networking Fundamentals
How to Be Remarkable
Personal Branding

Memoirs
Come Back Frayed
Iceland India Interstate
My Exile Lifestyle

Fiction Series
A Tale of More
Real Powers

Novels
Puncture Up
Ordovician

Short Fiction Collections
Coffee with the Other Man
So This Is How I Go
Mean Universe
7 or 8 Ways to End the World
7 or 8 More Ways to End the World

29051761R00185

Made in the USA
Middletown, DE
04 February 2016